ALL OUR
TRAGIC

PART II
POLITICS

This is a work of fiction. All of the characters, events, and organizations portrayed in this work are either products of the author's imagination or used fictitiously.

All Our Tragic

Adapted from the plays of antiquity

ISBN-13: 978-1957328157

For production information,
contact sean@seangraney.com

Cover art by Kate Carson-Groner

Published by Sordelet Ink
WWW.SORDELETINK.COM

ALL OUR TRAGIC

A PLAY BY
SEAN GRANEY

A CONTEMPORARY FESTIVAL OF DIONYSUS,
A DAY-LONG PLAY RETELLING OF THE
THIRTY-TWO SURVIVING GREEK TRAGEDIES.

PART II
POLITICS

SORDELET Ink

ALL OUR TRAGIC

KEY TO ORIGINAL TRAGEDIES

AESCHYLUS
AGAMEMNON (AGAMEMNON)
FURIES (Section of THE FURIES)
LIBATION BEARERS (Part of the conglomerate ELEKTRA)
PROMETHEUS BOUND (PROMETHEUS)
SEVEN AGAINST THEBES
   (Part of the conglomerate .07 AGAINST THEBES)
SUPPLIANTS (THE SEVEN SISTERS)
THE PERSIANS (A mention in PROMETHEUS)
(Poetry from THE PERSIANS inspired WARDAYS and
   THE END BEGINS)

SOPHOCLES
AJAX (OLD-FASHIONED HONOR: AJAX)
ANTIGONE (ANTIGONE)
ELECTRA (Part of the conglomerate ELEKTRA)
OEDIPUS AT COLONUS (THE MAUSOLEUM)
OEDIPUS THE KING (ŒDIPUS)
PHILOCTETES (OLD-FASHIONED HONOR: ΦILOKTETES)
WOMEN OF TRACHIS (LABORS AND LIES, EPISODE TWO:
   LIES)

EURIPIDES
ALCESTIS (ALKESTIS)
ANDROMACHE (Section of THE FURIES)
ELECTRA (Part of the conglomerate ELEKTRA)
HECUBA (Part of the conglomerate HECUBA TROYFALL)
HELEN (HELEN)
HERACLEIDAE (AFTER HERAKLES)
HERACLES (RAGE HERAKLES, RAGE)
HIPPOLYTUS (PHÈDRE)
ION (ION)
IPHIGENIA IN AULIS (IPHIGENIA)
IPHIGENIA IN TAURIS (Section of THE FURIES)
MEDEA (MÉDÉE)
ORESTES (Section of THE FURIES)
RHESUS (THE TROJANS)
SUPPLIANTS (THE SUPPLIANT)
THE BACCHAE (BACCHAE)
THE PHOENICIAN WOMEN (Part of the conglomerate .07 AGAINST
   THEBES)
THE TROJAN WOMEN (Part of the conglomerate HECUBA
   TROYFALL)
For a bonus, Euripides' satyr play—**THE CYCLOPS** (Part of THE
   SEVEN SISTERS)

VERY SPECIAL PATRONS:
THIS SCRIPT WOULD NOT BE POSSIBLE
WITHOUT THE UNBELIEVABLE LOVE AND
SUPPORT OF JOHN, STEPH, AND LEVI
TIPTON. I AM FOREVER THANKFUL TO
YOUR AMAZING FAMILY.

AND AS ALWAYS SPECIAL THANKS TO MY
ARTISTIC HOME, THE HYPOCRITES.

In Loving Memory of
Erin Myers

ALL OUR TRAGIC was first produced on August 10th, 2014 by THE HYPOCRITES (Artistic Director, Halena Kays; Managing Director, Megan Wildebour) at the Den Theater, Chicago, IL, USA. It was directed by Sean Graney.

ORIGINAL PRODUCTION TEAM
Miranda Anderson, Stage Manager; Pat Fries and Amanda Clayton Production Managers; Justine Palmisano and Casey Peek Assistant Stage Managers; Thrisa Hodits, Second Director; Chloe Dzielak and Evan Garrett Assistant Directors; Ryan Bourque, Violence Choreographer; Alison Siple, Costume Designer; Tom Burch, Set Designer; Danielle Case, Prop Designer; Jared Moore, Light Designer; Kevin O'Donnell, Sound Designer; Mieka van der Ploeg, Wigs, Make up and Assistant Costume Designer; Crystal Mormen, Gore Designer; Jon Beal, Blood Specialist and Assistant Fight Designer.

ORIGINAL CAST
Erin Myers ODD-JOB ALICE
Lauren Vogel ODD-JOB SOPHIE
Kate Carson-Groner ODD-JOB ERDIE
Dana Omar MÉDÉE, CREUSA, KALCHAS, COUSIN DOLON
Emily Casey MOUSE, AGAVE, HELEN
Lindsey Gavel ALKESTIS, TIRESIAS, IPHIGENIA, ELEKTRA
Tien Doman KLYTAIMNĒSTRA, DEJANIRA, ODYSSA, GLAUKE
Erin Barlow ASTEROPE, ANTIGONE, POLYXENA, HERMIONE
Christine Stulik PHÆDRE, CTESSIPOS, JOKASTA, KASSANDRA
Ryan Bourque THESEUS, LYNCEUS, MENELAUS
Maximillian Lapine EURYSTHEUS, POLYNIKES, AJAX
Danny Goodman ΦILOKTETES, CADMUS, HECTOR, AIGISTHOS
Luce Metrius JASON, HÆMON, GROUCHY GLENUS, ACHILLES
Zeke Sulkes ÆGEUS, KREON, NEOPTOLEMUS
John Taflan PATROKLOS, OEDIPUS, PYLADES
Walter Briggs HERAKLES, PENTHEUS THE GAUNT, AGAMEMNON
Geoff Button PROMETHEUS, ETEOKLES, ORESTES
(Breon Arzell, Will Bennett, Christopher Bryant, Rashaad Hall, Danny Martinez, Kevin Reyes)

Many contributed time and talent without whom the show would not have opened.

Cast Breakdown

ODD-JOB ALICE

ODD-JOB SOAPY

ODD-JOB ERDIE

1: MÉDÉE, CREUSA, ETEOKLES, HECUBA, AMAZON, SHEEP, ELEKTRA, IPHIGENIA/BUTCHER PRIESTESS

2: PHÆDRE, ASTEROPE, CTESSIPOS, JOKASTA, KAPANEÚS, KASSANDRA

3: THÍBA, DEJANIRA, ODYSSA/EWE, KLYTAIMNĒSTRA

4: GLAUKE, MOUSE, ANTIGONE, POLYXENA, SHEEP, HERMIONE/'POLYXENA'

5: ALKESTIS, TIRESIAS, TYDEUS, KALCHAS, HELEN/HELÉN, PENTHESILEA, SHEEP

6: HERAKLES/NŌMAN, PENTHEUS THE GAUNT, AGAMEMNON/RAM

7: THESEUS, LYNCEUS, MENELAUS/LAMB, BATHYKLES

8: EURYSTHEUS, POLYNIKES, BIG BROTHER, RHESUS, AJAX, AIGISTHOS

9: ΦILOKTETES, HIPPOLYTUS' VOICE, CADMUS, UNKNOWN TROJAN, TROILUS, BAT TZAR OF BATS

10: JASON, CYKLOPS, GROUCHY GLENUS, ION/HÆMON, .07er, ACHILLES, SHEEP, CIVILIAN, LITTLE BROTHER, PYLADES/ORDERLY

11: ÆGEUS, CYKLOPS, PATROKLOS, KREON, NEOPTOLEMUS

12: PROMETHEUS, CYKLOPS, ŒDIPUS, .07er, SHEEP, HECTOR, ORESTES/DEPUTY/÷

Note: names should be pronounced how the audience is accustomed to hearing them, even if the names are spelled with Greek or linguistic accent marks. Therefore, MÉDÉE is pronounced like the typical MEDEA, PHÆDRE is pronounced like the typical PHAEDRA, and HELÉN is pronounced like the typical HELEN.

ALL OUR TRAGIC SETTING

This is like a factory that makes nothing and everything.

It is like an office built for something else.

It is old and just gets older.

It has a raised platform with three swinging doors,

A large metal sliding door,

A metal trap door in the floor,

A sunken area, upstage, with three chairs and musical instruments, for the Odd-Jobs to watch the entire show.

In this Odd-Job pit is a very large blackboard

With a library ladder:

On which Odd-Jobs keep a Death Tally in the center.

The Odd-Jobs also write character names as they enter,

And cross them out with red chalk when they die.

Also, as they hear lines,

They write quotes from the show at their discretion,

Ideally these quotes should be very small,

Only to be read by the audience during intermission,

And these can vary slightly every performance.

Finally, to make a happier Odd-Job and audience experience.

Please allow the Odd-Jobs to have some artistic freedom,

To draw pictures or frames around different sections,

Or generally creating an incredibly crafty blackboard.

During breaks, please invite the audience on the set,

To sit, eat food, stretch out, look at the blackboard,

And most importantly talk to each other and the actors.

THOUGHTS ON PERFORMANCE

ALL OUR TRAGIC is written to be performed in a single day. It takes ten to twelve hours.

It is crafted to have many intermissions and extended food breaks:

Each part contains a fifteen-minute intermission.

Between Part 1 and Part 2 there is a thirty-minute lunch break.

Between Part 2 and Part 3 there is an hourlong dinner break.

Between Part 3 and Part 4 there is a thirty-minute dessert break.

Despite how this script is formatted, ALL OUR TRAGIC is not meant to be a cycle-play, to be broken into sections and performed over the course of many evenings. It works best as a single play with a continuous narrative.

During intermissions, food is always available. Please encourage the audience to occupy the space, to sit on the stage and have conversations. Let them explore the space as theirs. It is great when the performers join the audience for meals.

ALL OUR TRAGIC
SPECIAL ACKNOWLEDGMENTS

ALL OUR TRAGIC was developed at the Radcliffe Institute for Advanced Study and the Getty Villa Lab.

It would not be possible without the unbelievable love and support of Ed Sylvanus Iskandar and Exit, Pursued by a Bear, as well as incredible generosity from hundreds of special benefactors. Including, but not limited to Craig Steadman, Shawn Donnelley, Will Forrest, Dave Wimsatt, Ernst Malchior, Bart Lazar, Jack and Linda Doman, Carol Ostrow, Robin Tennant Colburn, Karen Van Metere, David Westby, and numerous other generous financial contributors.

This script reflects the creative voices of countless talented individuals from American Repertory Theater/Moscow Art Theater School, Institute for Advanced Theater Training at Harvard University (with dramaturgy by Morgan Goldstein), Illinois State University, Lake Forest College, DePaul University and University of Chicago.

ALL OUR TRAGIC

PART II
POLITICS

PROLOGUE

(Blackboard review—the only names that should be in tact are ΦILOKTETES, PATROKLOS, CADMUS, THESEUS, JASON and four of SEVEN SISTERS: CREUSA, THÍBA, KLYTAIMNĒSTRA and HELEN; the Death Tally should be twenty)

(ODD-JOB ALICE enters. She wears a classic housekeeping dress, like from a hotel, and carries a guitar, or some other musical instrument)

ODD-JOB ALICE
Another day.

(ODD-JOB SOAPY enters wearing an identical uniform and carrying another guitar)

ODD-JOB SOAPY
Odd-Job Alice, good to see you.

ODD-JOB ALICE
You too, Odd-Job Soapy.

ODD-JOB SOAPY
The new one back yet?

(ODD-JOB ERDIE enters)

ODD-JOB ERDIE
You talking about me?

ODD-JOB SOAPY
Time to announce and sing,
And a few other things.

ODD-JOB ERDIE
I'm excited.
What's next?

ODD-JOB ALICE
Part 2: Politics.

ODD-JOB SOAPY
Twenty-five years after the last section.

ODD-JOB ERDIE
Hold on, I've got the perfect thing once again.

(ODD-JOB ERDIE exits and enters with a triangle. The ODD-JOBS sing)

[THE SONG ABOUT ACT 3 AND ITS COMPLICATIONS]

ACT III

(ODD-JOB ALICE opens a big sliding door. KREON enters, drinking some Dragon-Head Coffee® out of a paper-cup. The song ends)

ODD-JOB ERDIE
You sounded great.

ODD-JOB SOAPY
Thanks.
Year 45.

ODD-JOB ERDIE
The Bacchae.

(The ODD-JOBS gets settled at their station and work on the blackboard again)

KREON
I love this time of day,
When the sun wraps the city in a soft glow,
The city becomes us,
And we become the city.
It makes one happy to be a citizen.

(Enter ANTIGONE)

ANTIGONE
Merry Dragon Day, Uncle Kreon.

KREON
Merry Dragon Day, Antigone.

ANTIGONE
All of Thebes is gathered for the Dragon Day Speech.

KREON
It seems so,
And unfortunately, we can't find my father.

ANTIGONE
But Grandpa Cadmus has to talk in maybe twenty minutes.

KREON
Five, five minutes.
He'll be here.
The whole family is looking for him.

ANTIGONE
It seems like he's apathetic toward being king.

KREON
Your grandfather Cadmus loved being the leader of Thebes,
When it was a quaint commune he named after Thíba.
But thirty years ago he buried Médée's Dragon,
Then Thebes grew quickly into the massive complicated city it is.
Thíba tries to keep him engaged,
But Cadmus hates the political necessities of a good ruler.

ANTIGONE
I guess that makes sense to me.
If an action causes you to lose connection to individuals,
Why do it?

KREON
I think politics might be a little more complicated than that, Antigone.

ANTIGONE
Then again, maybe it's not, Kreon.

(Enter JOKASTA urgently, drinking some Dragon-Head Coffee® out of a paper-cup carrying the Coat of Thebes)

JOKASTA
Thíba found Cadmus.

KREON
Thank goodness, Jokasta.

ANTIGONE
Where was he, mother?

JOKASTA
Sitting by the river in his bathrobe drinking lemonade,
Talking to a scamp.

ANTIGONE
Sounds nice.

JOKASTA
No Antigone, nice?
My father has to deliver the most important speech in our city's existence.

(ŒDIPUS enters drinking some Dragon-Head Coffee®, he kisses JOKASTA)

ŒDIPUS
Cadmus ready?

JOKASTA
Thíba just found him, Œdipus.

ŒDIPUS
He has to get out in front of the people, they're getting antsy.
Oh, I'm a mess, I spilled my Dragon-Head®. *(Wipes off some coffee spill)*

KREON
Merry Dragon Day, Œdipus.

ŒDIPUS
Merry Dragon Day, buddy.

ANTIGONE
Dad, you ran off fast, you forgot your lunch.

(ANTIGONE gives ŒDIPUS a bagged lunch)

KREON
You spoil your father.

ANTIGONE
There might be a Dragon Day treat in there for you, Uncle.

(ŒDIPUS pulls out a snack bag and throws it to KREON)

ŒDIPUS
Cheezee-Q's®.

KREON
I love Cheezee-Q's®.

ANTIGONE
Sorry Mom, I didn't bring you anything.

JOKASTA
Good, I don't want anything.

ANTIGONE
Good.

ŒDIPUS
Okay. Get out of here, Antigone.
Make sure the twins get their breakfast.

ANTIGONE
I'm younger than them.

ŒDIPUS
But more responsible.
Love you.

(ANTIGONE exits)

JOKASTA
That girl has problems.

ŒDIPUS
Only if you find greatness a problem.

(Enter PENTHEUS THE GAUNT)

PENTHEUS THE GAUNT
Where are they?

JOKASTA
Pentheus the Gaunt, did Thíba lose Cadmus?

PENTHEUS THE GAUNT
No, my Mumsie was dressing him,
But they should be done.
How long does it take for a grown man to get dressed?

KREON
Everything is too much for Father,
The way Thebes is now breaks his heart.

PENTHEUS THE GAUNT
Then heck, I'll lead.
Give me the ruling Coat of Thebes right now,
Know what I'm saying?

JOKASTA
Pentheus the Gaunt, you would be the worst ruler,
Babies would even rebel.

PENTHEUS THE GAUNT
Oh, half-sister, I would make a better ruler than you or
your dumb, young husband.

ŒDIPUS
Crackity crickets, I'm standing right here.

*(Enter THÍBA, with her umbrella, dressing CADMUS
sipping on a glass of lemonade)*

THÍBA
Come on Cadmus,
Just tie the tie.

CADMUS
I don't want to tie the tie, Thíba.

THÍBA
You have to, it's Dragon Day,
You have to give the Dragon Day speech.
Just tie the tie!

CADMUS
One more sip of lemonade.

THÍBA
Tie the tie or I will tie it so tightly you will never drink
lemonade again!

CADMUS
Okay Thíba, you're right.
Thanks for taking care of things.

THÍBA
I love you!

CADMUS
I love you, Seven Sister!
Here, Pentheus the Gaunt, hold my lemonade.

PENTHEUS THE GAUNT
A pleasure to be helpful, Father.

(CADMUS hands his lemonade to PENTHEUS THE GAUNT and ties his tie)

ŒDIPUS
Merry Dragon Day, Cadmus.

CADMUS
Hey Œdipus,
Class act, right here, class act,
This guy solved the Riddle of the Hellbitch.

KREON
That was fantastic.

CADMUS
How are my grandkids?

ŒDIPUS
Antigone is still quite a sunny young woman.

JOKASTA
No she's not, she broods a lot.

CADMUS
And the twins?

ŒDIPUS
Polynikes acts like Eteokles and Eteokles like Polynikes.

CADMUS
And the other child?

ŒDIPUS
Just the three, sir.

CADMUS
I swear, man, ain't there another one.

JOKASTA
Dad, I did have a baby with my first husband,
But that baby died in infancy over thirty years ago.

CADMUS
Son of a—what is happening with my mind?
I'm so sorry, Jokasta, I forgot.
I really wish that ruling Thebes didn't take so much effort,
I want to just hang out more with everyone.

PENTHEUS THE GAUNT
Even me, Father?

CADMUS
Sure, why not, Pentheus the Gaunt.

PENTHEUS THE GAUNT
You know, Father,
You don't have to call me Pentheus the Gaunt.

CADMUS
{Thíba, didn't we name him Pentheus the Gaunt.}

THÍBA
{We just named him Pentheus,
The Gaunt part developed over time.}

PENTHEUS THE GAUNT
If you get too tired and want to give up the ruling Coat
of...

CADMUS
All dressed.
Who's got my speech?

KREON
I do Father.

(KREON gives CADMUS a typed speech)

CADMUS
Did you write this, Kreon?

KREON
Yes sir.

CADMUS
Why did you put it on smelly paper, man?

KREON
I didn't notice.

CADMUS
It's like gouda.
Hey Kreon, I was just talking with this admirable drifter,
She asked me a theoretical question,
Is it best to be friendly, feared or faithful?
What do you think?

KREON
I'm not sure, sir.

THÍBA
What are you talking about?
You have to go give the Dragon Day speech, Cadmus.

CADMUS
Jokasta, help me with the ruling Coat of Thebes.

(JOKASTA puts the Coat on CADMUS)

JOKASTA
You still got it, sir.

CADMUS
I ain't ever had it, Jojo.
Okay, where do I start the speech?

KREON
(Pointing on the paper) My fellow Thebans.

CADMUS
(Smelling the paper) Classic opening.

KREON
Yes sir.

CADMUS *(Reading)*
Forty-five years ago, I started Thebes as a small
    encampment and named it after my fearless queen, Thíba.
Then to show that violence can be vanquished,
And calmness encouraged, I killed and buried a Dragon.
Blah blah Bacchac, blah blah plague, blah blah rebellion.
But still amidst all the troubles, Merry Dragon Day Thebes."
Then fireworks and that parade,
Where Polynikes and Eteokles dance under that rug,
Pretending to be a Dragon.
Man, where's my lemonade?

THÍBA
Cadmus, you have to read the whole speech

KREON
It's important.

CADMUS
What's important, Kreon, important what?
Someone get me my lemonade.

PENTHEUS THE GAUNT
Here it is, Father.

CADMUS
Did you spit in this?

PENTHEUS THE GAUNT
No.

THÍBA
Cadmus, you must address the problems of Thebes.

KREON
As outlined in my speech.

CADMUS
What problems?

THÍBA
They are legion, husband.

KREON
Two main ones. The population is growing so quickly...

CADMUS
It ain't my fault!
I wish I could have stopped it growing twenty-years ago.

KREON
I know father, but you didn't,
So now masses of people abandon their nomadic life and
  flock to urban Thebes,
Our unhappy population doubles every year,
Which gave rise to the Fox!

CADMUS
Aw man, foxes are so cute,
They're like dog AND cats.

KREON
No, Father, the Fox is the symbol for a new militia enlisting
  many citizens of Thebes.
They are called the Bacchae.

CADMUS
What type of politics do these Bacchae Foxes promote?

KREON
The best way to describe the Bacchae,
Is they are Anti... Anti...

THÍBA
You, dear, it's Anti-You.

PENTHEUS THE GAUNT
These angry asses convene within cabalistic covens, get
    uproariously inebriated,
Then demand the abolition of Government,
Like Theseus is doing with his Democratic States of Athens.

CADMUS
I met Theseus once, when his father goat died,
That was the day I slingshotted Médée's dragon, pshew!
Remember that, Honey?

THÍBA
I do.

CADMUS
Theseus, he seemed like a nice guy,
What's he up to?

THÍBA
How can you not know this, Cadmus?
He established a government that gives the ruling-power to
    the people,
He welcomes any city that wants to join him.

CADMUS
People with power,
That sounds like chaos.

PENTHEUS THE GAUNT
That's what the Bacchae want!

KREON
Actually, Father, you're getting fake information, here.
Theseus' Democracy is incredibly successful,
Athens is happy and productive.
Your manner of governing Thebes is causing chaos,
Just making up laws as you go.

CADMUS
Son of a—you sassing me, Kreon?

KREON
No sir, your casual rule was great when you could know all
  your neighbors,
But it isn't effective anymore,
Thebes is too big.

CADMUS
Your face is too big.

KREON
Okay. Also the Bacchae do not call for Democracy,
Their Fox symbol stands for the complete dissolution of
  Government.

PENTHEUS THE GAUNT
Father, give me the Coat of Thebes, I will stop these
  Bacchae Foxes,
Make each one of them suffer.

THÍBA
Really, son? How in the world would you expect to curb the
  Bacchae?

PENTHEUS THE GAUNT
I'll post an edict criminalizing any activity,
Then I'll infiltrate their little group at this Dragon Day
  speech and arrest a pivotal player.

CADMUS
Fine.

PENTHEUS THE GAUNT
What do you mean, "fine?"

CADMUS
Just go, Gaunt, do whatever you want.

PENTHEUS THE GAUNT
Really?

CADMUS
Yeah, what do I care?

PENTHEUS THE GAUNT
Then expect the fall of the Bacchae.
You will be proud of me sir.

CADMUS
I doubt it.

THÍBA
Pentheus, be smart,
And be cautious.

PENTHEUS THE GAUNT
Good rulers are neither, Mother.

(Exit PENTHEUS THE GAUNT)

KREON
The other problem Father is the Green Plague.

CADMUS
Is Green Plague as gross as it sounds, man?

KREON
Green Plague spreads like fire,
In the poorer sections of Thebes,
Some citizens don't have access to fresh water, healthy food,
  medical help.
It's a disaster down there,
And more and more people keep moving, jamming
themselves into this city.

CADMUS
Do troubles ever end?

ŒDIPUS
Cadmus, cross Green Plague off your list.
Your daughter and I can deal with it.
Which in turn, will probably calm the Bacchae rebellion.

JOKASTA
Why do we think we can do that?

ŒDIPUS
I solved the riddle of the Hellbitch.

KREON
That was fantastic.

CADMUS
Son of a—fine, go on, cure the Green Plague.
What do I care?

JOKASTA
Okay.

(Exit JOKASTA and ŒDIPUS)

CADMUS
Kreon, how 'bout it, son?
What would you do to get Thebes out of this foul mess?

KREON
I would ensure all citizens were informed of the laws.

CADMUS
Fine, I'm exhausted to death.
So tell all my children,
The first one to accomplish what they claim can take the
  Coat of Thebes from me.
I'm giving this dumb Dragon Day speech,
Then going back to bed, where I belong.
Merry Dragon Day.
I'm just thankful this is the last speech I give to this burden
  of a city.

(Exit CADMUS)

KREON
It's a strange Dragon Day, Thíba.

THÍBA
Indeed.
I should go make sure Cadmus stays on message.

KREON
Stepmother, I know this city thrives solely because of you,
Thebes not only bears your name, but your sweat and smarts.
So thank you.

THÍBA
When you get the Coat of Thebes,
You'll rule just as well.

KREON
I'm not sure politics suits me, Thíba.
I feel at the core of leadership
Lies a kernel that bolsters a leader to feel more important
   than the people he leads.
I don't really feel worthier than anyone.

THÍBA
I think you're right, but I just never thought of leadership
   like that.
A leader must feel entitled,
But act like she's not.
It's truly the nature of hierarchy,
And without hierarchy,
We have anarchy.

KREON
It gets confusing, Seven Sister.

THÍBA
Tell me about it.

That reminds me,
My Seven Sister Creusa, the boring one,
She's been Queen of the Isthmus since Glauke was eaten
  by the Colossal Eagle.
Anyway, she made a deal with Cadmus,
She wants to further merge our royal bloodlines,
So Cadmus volunteered you.

KREON
You mean,
I'm like going to be an arranged husband?

THÍBA
So says Cadmus.
It'll be good for Thebes, bolster our alliances.
You'll need to head off to Creusa at the Isthmus soon.

KREON
Then I would be your brother-in-law, step-son?

THÍBA
Don't look that deeply into it.

(Exit THÍBA. Enter PENTHEUS THE GAUNT, dressed
as a giant fox)

PENTHEUS THE GAUNT
To catch a Fox! Be a Fox!

KREON
Pentheus, did you just have that outfit lying around?

PENTHEUS THE GAUNT
After I posted the edicts banning the Bacchae,
I donned this disguise and watched for agitated dissenters.
This one fell right in to my trap.

(PENTHEUS THE GAUNT reaches off stage and grabs
TIRESIAS, who has her hands bound)

KREON
Tiresias, is that you?

TIRESIAS
Kreon?

PENTHEUS THE GAUNT
You know this rebel?

KREON
When we were younger,
Tiresias and I dated.

PENTHEUS THE GAUNT
Well, she is now a Fox,
I caught her loitering with her clique-claque at the Dragon
   Day speech.

TIRESIAS
Prince Pentheus, I think the Bacchae are as dangerous as
   you do.
They are too violent, wanting Cadmus to abdicate the Coat
   of Thebes,
I decided to not join the movement,
I have no interest in a coup.
I thought I might find hope in the betterment being
   preached by the Bacchae.
I can't hold a job.
My boy and I were just evicted.

KREON
Why didn't you let me know?

TIRESIAS
Was I supposed to write you a letter?
Dear Kreon, since you broke my heart,
Ion and I live in sewers.
Truly, Tiresias.

KREON
We were so young, I just couldn't have raised Ion with you.

PENTHEUS THE GAUNT
Kreon, you let this vagabond raise your royal bastardo?

KREON
No, Ion's not my son. We found him.

TIRESIAS
The cutest baby boy abandoned outside of a museum in a
  stewpot.

KREON
After a few days of searching for his parents,
Tiresias told me she wanted to adopt him with or without me.
So I left them.

PENTHEUS THE GAUNT
Perfect cad move, Kreon.

KREON
Come on, Tiresias, let's get you to your boy.

PENTHEUS THE GAUNT
Brother, I warn you, this Bachhae Fox is my prisoner and
  you may not have custody.

(Enter ION wearing a stewpot as a hat, carrying a tortoise)

ION
Tiresias!

TIRESIAS
Ion, you shouldn't be here.

KREON
What do you have there, Ion?

ION
During the Dragon Day speech a man sold me this baby dragon.

I'll love him and name him Cadmusaurus,
In honor of our royal founder,
Roar!

KREON
I don't think that's a baby dragon,
I think its a tortoise.

ION
Hold on, are you Prince Kreon?
Nanny has your pictures hidden in some books.

TIRESIAS
No need to talk about that, Ion.
But Nanny is in a little trouble right now, wait for me
  outside, okay.

ION
Yes Nanny.
Maybie, I'll run into Princess Antigone too!

(ION exits)

PENTHEUS THE GAUNT
Tiresias, who is the leader of the Bacchae?

TIRESIAS
I don't know.

PENTHEUS THE GAUNT
Then it's time for torture and maybe death.

KREON
Thebes is a civilized city,
We can't torture and execute people.

PENTHEUS THE GAUNT
Who can torture and execute people if not civilized cities?

(ANTIGONE runs on)

ANTIGONE
Uncle Kreon, Uncle Kreon!
At the Dragon Day speech, the Bacchae discovered
  Pentheus' edict banning them.
They started to chant over Grandpa Cadmus' voice,
"Kill the tyrants of Thebes! Long live the Bacchae!"
Grandpa became so frustrated, he toppled the podium, tore
  off his tie,
And went back to bed.
This pushed the Bacchae over the edge of sanity,
"Kill the tyrants of Thebes! Long live the Bacchae!"

TIRESIAS
Pentheus, heed my advice.

PENTHEUS THE GAUNT
No, Tiresias, the counsel of a hobo is of no use to a Prince!

TIRESIAS
Sense can only be sipped by those who thirst for it.

PENTHEUS THE GAUNT
The Age of Compromise in this city is over,
That was the old days of my father Cadmus' regime.
And that is why soon, I will clothe myself in the Ruling Coat.

KREON
Antigone, go find Seven Sister Thíba,
If anyone can calm the Bacchae she can.

ANTIGONE
Here she comes, how convenient.

(Enter THÍBA with THESEUS, wearing the Minotaur horns
on his back. THESEUS carries a big milk can)

THÍBA
I am afraid, Theseus, you caught Thebes at a really
  frenetic time,
But I'll try to find King Cadmus.

THESEUS
I appreciate it, Seven Sister.

THÍBA
Son, what are you doing?

PENTHEUS THE GAUNT
Establishing order.

THÍBA
As a stuffed animal?

PENTHEUS THE GAUNT
I'm in-fox-cognito, Mumsie.

THÍBA
(To TIRESIAS) Are you alright, lady?

TIRESIAS
I hope so, Queen.

PENTHEUS THE GAUNT
Who's this guy?

THESEUS
I'm Theseus, Ruler of the Democratic States of Athens.

THÍBA
I'll go get Cadmus, sir.
{Son, do not do anything foolish.
Theseus is the most powerful person in all the land.
He could destroy Thebes easily.
And I wish you picked a better day to publicly reveal your
  furry proclivities.}
One second Theseus.

ANTIGONE
Thíba, if you're trying to find Grandpa Cadmus, he went
  back to bed.

THÍBA
Of course he did,
Thank you Antigone.

(Exit THÍBA)

PENTHEUS THE GAUNT
So, you're the man uniting all of the cities,
The powerful Theseus.

THESEUS
I'm Theseus, not sure about the powerful part,
I just desire to do what's best for people,
So I let them tell me what they want.

KREON
It's admirable, sir.
I'm Kreon, a son of Cadmus.

ANTIGONE
Antigone, Cadmus' granddaughter.

TIRESIAS
Tiresias, down on my luck.

THESEUS
Nice to meet you all.

PENTHEUS THE GAUNT
I can field any traffic you have for my father, mighty
   Theseus.

KREON
Excuse us, King Theseus.
{Pentheus, half-brother, don't be a half-wit, let Father deal
   with this man.}

PENTHEUS THE GAUNT
{Before or after Father gets on his slippers. Step off, Kreon.}
King Theseus, what can I help you with?

THESEUS
Well, Pentheus the Gaunt, a group of angry Thebans came
    to Athens,
Passing out this propaganda.

*(THESEUS gives a small flag with a fox logo to PENTHEUS
THE GAUNT)*

PENTHEUS THE GAUNT
"Back us Bacchae!"

THESEUS
Then your Bacchae offered sips of this liquor.

(THESEUS shows the milk tin)

ANTIGONE
The Bacchae were drinking from cans like that at the
    speech.

TIRESIAS
A fearful alcoholic brew they call Vixen Milk.

THESEUS
So toxic, it actually caused a few of our young girls to go
    blind.
And the worst news yet,
The Bacchae also infected Athens with your viral Green
    Plague.
I'm all for Free Speech and rightful protest.
In Athens, we have quite a few gatherings against me.
Conversations and compromise lead to betterment.
But this group of Bacchae has bloody intentions to remove
    the rights of others.
So, I come to Thebes, to request you do something about
    this group of bigots,
To appease my Athenians.

PENTHEUS THE GAUNT
Appease you?

THESEUS
Yes, appease my Athenians.

PENTHEUS THE GAUNT
Thebes might not be interested in appeasing a political bully,
Like all the other cowardly cities.

THESEUS
Is that so?

KREON
{Make not this meeting sour, Pentheus the Gaunt.}

(Enter THÍBA)

THÍBA
King Theseus, my husband, Cadmus, will be here shortly,
He's just putting on some pants. I apologize for the wait.

THESEUS
No apologies needed, Queen Thíba,
I'm finding this conversation quite entertaining.

PENTHEUS THE GAUNT
So I amuse you, sir?

THESEUS
Yes sir, you do, sir.

PENTHEUS THE GAUNT
Then maybe your laughter,
Can keep you company back to Athens.

THÍBA
Please excuse my foolish boy, King Theseus.

PENTHEUS THE GAUNT
You think I'm a fool, Mumsie?

THÍBA
Well, who does foolish things aside from fools, son?

PENTHEUS THE GAUNT
You will see, I am no fool,
I'll show, I'm fit to rule.

THESEUS
Fine, Pentheus the Gaunt, what can your Thebes do for Athens?

PENTHEUS THE GAUNT
What did you say happened when Athenians drank that hooch?

THESEUS
Some women lost their sight.

(PENTHEUS THE GAUNT waves the little propaganda flag)

PENTHEUS THE GAUNT
Tiresias, you're a member of the Bacchae.

TIRESIAS
As I have said over and over again,
I was for one night.

PENTHEUS THE GAUNT
Theseus, to appease Athens, as apparently a great leader should,
Bacchae shall be punished in a manner which they've caused,
One eye gone for one eye lost.

(With the propaganda flag, PENTHEUS THE GAUNT repeatedly stabs TIRESIAS in the eyes. KREON stops him. THÍBA and ANTIGONE help her, wrapping her eyes in a scarf)

TIRESIAS
Pity, please.
Help!

THÍBA
Oh my son, my son,
What have you done?

PENTHEUS THE GAUNT
I have appeased all-powerful Athens.

THESEUS
Whoa man, I meant like some community service or a fine.

TIRESIAS
My eyes, are they gone?
Are they gone?

PENTHEUS THE GAUNT
Yes, Tiresias, I just blinded you.

TIRESIAS
Why can I see, without my eyes, why can I see?

PENTHEUS THE GAUNT
You can't, that's the point of blinding.

THÍBA
Please, go King Theseus, I'm sorry.
Let my family regulate our family problems,
Then I promise there will be reparations.

THESEUS
Fine, Thíba, but if Cadmus gives Pentheus the ruling coat,
Cadmus is giving Thebes complications with Athens.

(THÍBA takes the bottle from THESEUS, he exits)

THÍBA
Son, what have you become?

PENTHEUS THE GAUNT
I admit, I'm a little surprised myself I did that.
But to be a mighty city Thebes needs a mighty ruler.

THÍBA
You're destroying my city.

PENTHEUS THE GAUNT
I'm making her great.

KREON
No, Gaunt, you are a Dragon.

PENTHEUS THE GAUNT
Sure, I've been a Dragon,
Like Médée's buried in the center of town,
The symbol father wanted us to worship.

THÍBA
Cadmus wanted us to see the greatness of humanity,
Destroying ferocity.

PENTHEUS THE GAUNT
Please, Mumsie, we only saw the greatness of ferocity,
And fiercely, I acted for the advancement of all.

KREON
You acted for the advancement of one.

THÍBA
Cadmus will never give you the Coat of Thebes.

PENTHEUS THE GAUNT
Father's days are over.
He dreamt of prosperity
But that is the only thing he did, dream,
While sipping lemonade in slippers.
"Wouldn't it be great if Thebes was incredible."
Yes, it would, Dad, yes it would!

But he wouldn't do anything!
So I plotted and planned without Father knowing,
I made deals and urged growth, I did so with sheer
  determination,
I built walls to guard our industry and assets,
I made Thebes into the powerful city it is, I did!

KREON
You boastful fool, your mother did those deeds.

PENTHEUS THE GAUNT
No it was me, me, me!
And I will pay any price for protection and expansion, any.
And that is what will make me a great leader.
Cadmus is dead, or soon will be,
Long live Pentheus the Strong.
I will show Thebes the cost of being insolent,
This lady is not the last of the Bacchae that will suffer
  stripes and strokes.
Then, if Father will not bestow upon me the Coat of
  Thebes,
I will take it from his dead hairy back.

*(THÍBA hits PENTHEUS hard over the head with the bottle,
he tries to crawl away saying "Mumsie." THÍBA continues
to beat on him. ODD-JOBS sing)*

[THE SECOND SONG OF FILICIDE]

KREON
What are you doing, Thíba?

THÍBA
He can't be allowed to live, did you hear him?
Threatening to kill Cadmus, he has gone beyond forgivable.

ANTIGONE
She's going to kill her own son.

THÍBA
No, my son was killed when this maniac killed his
  compassion.
What I kill now is a usurping oppressor.
The Bacchae was right, "Kill the Tyrants of Thebes."
Now, Kreon, hold him for me, this task cannot be half-
  done.

KREON
Yes ma'am.

(KREON holds PENTHEUS)

THÍBA
Take this last opportunity to atone, despot.

PENTHEUS THE GAUNT
(Dying) Atone for my sins or yours, Mumsie?
Death is death is death is death.

(THÍBA kills PENTHEUS with the bottle. An ODD-JOB
stirkes his name and tallies his death)

THÍBA
Death and life,
Both terrible obligations.

KREON
Cadmus will kill you for that, Thíba.

THÍBA
Maybe he should.

(Enter ION, wearing his stewpot, carrying his tortoise)

ION
Cadmusaurus, close your dragon eyes.

TIRESIAS
Who's here?

ION
Your stewpot boy, Nanny.

(Enter ŒDIPUS and JOKASTA)

JOKASTA
What is this?

THÍBA
Come on in, be not shy,
Look upon what cannot look.
I smote the Tyrant of Thebes.

TIRESIAS
Is this Jokasta and Œdipus?

ŒDIPUS
Yes, we're here.

TIRESIAS
I see you, I see you,
Oh, it's not now, but then,
When came the foul mess.
Take me away,
What do I see,
How did that come?
Who knew?
Who knew about this child?
Her child, her first child,
Mark that, child, the child!
Who knew?

JOKASTA
Lady, you don't know what you're saying.

TIRESIAS
I don't know what I say but I know what I see.
A double brood of confused genetics,
Husband by a husband,

Children by a child.
Œdipus and Antigone,
On one line.
One point,
One line.

ANTIGONE
What does she mean Father?

ŒDIPUS
I don't know, Antigone. Stay back.

TIRESIAS
Half of you knew this day would come,
And the other half is for whom this day comes.
I must leave Thebes,
Rot, rot, to rot.
For I and she are friendly not.
The door, the door,
This is the door, no?

ION
No, here it is.

KREON
Ion, get Tiresias to a hospital.

TIRESIAS
I will see you all again.

(Exit ION guiding TIRESIAS)

JOKASTA
She'll never see us again.

KREON
How do you know?

JOKASTA
She has no eyes.

(Enter CADMUS)

CADMUS
Oh man, unhappy creatures see unhappy things.

ŒDIPUS
King Cadmus, no need to look.

CADMUS
Is that my youngest boy lifeless?
Is he gone, Thíba, is the boy we raised gone?

THÍBA
Yes, honey,
We raised the son,
But the man made himself a tyrant.
He blinded a woman,
He planned to do the same to hundreds of citizens.

KREON
He threatened you, father.
So Thíba stopped him.

CADMUS
Stopped him?

THÍBA
I killed Pentheus.

CADMUS
Are you insane, wife?

THÍBA
No, Cadmus, I silenced this usurper for the sake of justice.

CADMUS
Justice? Justice?
Call you this justice?

THÍBA
Cadmus, if you find my actions wrong,
If you think your wife a murderer,
Then perform justice on me,
If that's what you want.
Break the Seven Sister number order,
Break the curse.
Look.

(THÍBA holds out her arm covered with green pustules)

CADMUS
What is that, man?

THÍBA
Theban Green Plague.
Go on, husband, cure my illness,
If you want to start making laws, make justice on me.

CADMUS
Get your justice out of my face, woman,
I can't be a part of this shameful wreckage.
Who do you think I am?
My wife has killed my son,
And kill my wife, my love, for it,
How could I?
What man could?

THÍBA
You will see, it is easy, if you think it's just.

CADMUS
I have no idea what is just, sickened Seven Sister,
I guess I never learned your type of justice.
Let the next ruler ponder the justice in murder.
Kreon, take the Coat.

KREON
Father, I must admit, I helped Thíba.

CADMUS
You murdered your brother?

KREON
Partly, sir.

CADMUS
Go to the Isthmus, man, to Creusa, your boring Seven
  Sister bride,
If she'll still have you, go!
Thebes shall never again be home to thee.

KREON
Are you like banishing me?

CADMUS
Now!

KREON
Yes sir.

JOKASTA
Mind the Madness of the Wasteland, brother.

ANTIGONE
I'll see you out, uncle.

KREON
I'd like that, Antigone.

CADMUS
Go!
And think about this as you wander to the Isthmus,
Is it best to be friendly, feared or faithful?

(Exit KREON and ANTIGONE hand in hand)

THÍBA
Give me the Coat, Cadmus, let me rule this city that bears
  my name.

CADMUS
No way Thíba, you killed our son.
You'll never be more than you were this morning.
Jokasta, take the Coat of Thebes,
Share this baleful hair-shirt with your stupid husband.

(CADMUS gives the Coat of Thebes to JOKASTA)

JOKASTA
Thank you, sir.

CADMUS
Thank me?
For troubles?
Don't be dumb, Jo-Jo,
I raised you better than that.

JOKASTA
Yes sir.

ŒDIPUS
What will you do Cadmus?

CADMUS
Go outside the gates of Thebes,
Wander the Madness of the Wasteland to exemplify my
   disgust and isolation,
My life is now a memory of distaste.
Thíba, what happened, you used to be so cool?

THÍBA
I grew up, Cadmus, I grew up.
Like Thebes.

CADMUS
Is it best to be friendly, feared or faithful?
Good luck to the whole lot of you let-downs.

(Exit CADMUS. JOKASTA dons the Coat of Thebes)

JOKASTA
Yes!
We rule.

THÍBA
So, now Queen Jokasta, what's your verdict for this former
  Queen?
A life for a life?

JOKASTA
No Thíba, you're too smart to kill,
Be my emissary to the Bacchae,
Tell them tyranny in Thebes is dead before it began.

THÍBA
Thank you, my Queen.

(Exit THÍBA)

ŒDIPUS
Why so lenient on Thíba?

JOKASTA
Too much action causes too much friction.
Plus, my Seven Sister Stepmother has the Green Plague,
She won't last a week anyway.

ŒDIPUS
Coat looks good on you.

JOKASTA
Thanks.

ŒDIPUS
Honey, do you think the child mentioned by that blind lady,
Is the baby you lost with your first husband?

JOKASTA
Look at me, look at my eyes, Œdipoo,
That was so long ago make me not think on it.

We need to cure the plague to deliver Thebes into her
shining future, Husband.

ŒDIPUS
After all, I'm the man who solved the Riddle of the
Hellbitch.

JOKASTA
And I fell in love with you then.
Help me with my half-brother,
The people will want a funeral.

ŒDIPUS
Thebes does love to honor its dead.

JOKASTA
The dust of the past cannot settle without a burial.

*(Drums and lights! Enter under a Dragon costume, with
POLYNIKES dancing and puppeting the Dragon head,
ETEOKLES, dancing under the tail. The dance ends)*

POLYNIKES + ETEOKLES *(Under dragon)*
Merry Dragon Day!

JOKASTA
Eteokles, Polynikes,
Not now.

*(ŒDIPUS and JOKASTA exits with dead PENTHEUS
THE GAUNT. POLYNIKES and ETEOKLES take off the
costume)*

POLYNIKES
Isn't it still Dragon Day, Eteokles?

ETEOKLES
Who knows what problems possess these people this time.

(ETEOKLES and POLYNIKES exit)

ODD-JOB ERDIE
One year later,
Year 46: Ion.

(ION enters wearing his stewpot hat, carrying a mug, and his tortoise)

ION
Cadmusaurus, it sure is a hot one today in the Apartment
  Temple.

(ION sets up two fans. Enter THÍBA, with her umbrella, sick with more boils)

THÍBA
Ring-a-ring Ion, and his tortoise.

ION
Queen Thíba, is that you?

THÍBA
I know a year with the Green Plague makes me a little
  repulsive.

ION
Here's some water, Thíba?

(ION gives THÍBA the mug of water and points a fan at her)

ION
And some air too.

(TIRESIAS blind, enters)

TIRESIAS
  Whichever Plague carrier is with you, Ion, best be on
  their boots soon.

THÍBA
Sorry Tiresias, this is Thíba, I come as an emissary from
  the Bacchae.

They want you to read their future to see what action can
   overturn Queen Jokasta.

TIRESIAS
Am I supposed to give a group of rebels reason to rebel?
Tell all the Bacchae, if the don't carry the Green Plague,
They can come one at a time to hear their personal future
   for the right fee.

THÍBA
Yes, of course lady, thank you.

(THÍBA gives money to TIRESIAS, who holds the bill away
from her as if it is infected)

TIRESIAS
I'm not a charity,
If I take your money, you take your future.

THÍBA
Then let's hear it.

TIRESIAS
You get worse before you get better,
And better before you get worse.

THÍBA
That's like a trick, you just described everyone's life.

TIRESIAS
Did I?
How's this,
Just when you're at your best you'll get your worst.
Now, please scram, Green Queen.

(TIRESIAS shoves the bill into the mug THÍBA holds)

THÍBA
Okay, augur.
Here's your mug Ion.

TIRESIAS
Keep the mug, Lady Cadmus.

(THÍBA exits)

ION
I'll miss that mug with tigers,
It was my second favorite.

TIRESIAS
Well you shouldn't have shared it with a Plague victim.
It's a hot one up here.

(ION adjusts both fans to point at TIRESIAS)

ION
Thar she blows.

TIRESIAS
Ion, finding you as a babe in that stewpot was the best thing
   that happened to me.

ION
Thank you, Nanny.

TIRESIAS
No need to thank the one that receives the gift.

ION
Perhaps today you can read my future, I want to know if
   I'm destined for greatness.

TIRESIAS
I will not read your destiny.
But know, in youth we're all destined for greatness
Now before it gets too late,
I should slaughter the lamb in the bathtub
So I can read his guts,
Into the Oracle Room I go.

ION
Most people call it a bathroom.

TIRESIAS
Most people don't have an out-of-home prophecy business.

ION
Today is when the Seven Sister Queen of the Isthmus,
Creusa, will be here with her newlywed husband,
They're having problems conceiving a child.
We don't want a Queen to think our Oracle Room is stuffy
   and stinky.

TIRESIAS *(having a vision)*
Oh no!

ION
What is it Tiresias?

TIRESIAS
You have to take off your stewpot okay.
You're too old for it, let me take it.

ION
Okay.

*(ION gives TIRESIAS his stewpot, she quickly exits into the
bathroom with the stewpot. ANTIGONE enters)*

ANTIGONE
Hello Ion.

(ION adjusts a fan for ANTIGONE)

ION
Hi yo Antigone,
Have you come for your future reading?

ANTIGONE
Nope, why know in advance what you'll be living through?

It's hard enough living through things when you live
  through them,
Never mind living through the worry about living through
  them.

ION
That makes sense.
So what brings you up here?
Me?

ANTIGONE
I'm just getting some time away from the streets,
The Bacchae is getting a little agitated again.
Plus, I like the view from the windows up here,
You can see the dirt of the Maddening Wasteland.

ION
What girl likes dirt?

ANTIGONE
This one.

(CREUSA enters, a little breathless, with her umbrella)

CREUSA
Why is this apartment temple on the top floor of a high-rise
  with no lift.

ION
Tiresias likes to avoid the Theban Green Plague,
And casual shopping traffic.

ANTIGONE
I'll let you get back to work, Ion.
Oh, Thíba threw this mug away,
I thought you'd want it back.

(ANTIGONE gives ION the tiger mug and exits. ION adjusts
the fan for CREUSA)

CREUSA
No love like young love.

ION
Oh Antigone and I aren't in love,
At least she don't love me, tears.
Well, welcome to Tiresias' Apartment Temple,
The rules are simple here, "No food, drink or shoes in the
   Oracle Room {Bathroom},
And under no circumstance is violence to be performed."

(KREON enters eating Cheezee-Q's®. ION adjusts another fan for KREON)

KREON
I love this new flavor of Cheezee-Q's®.

CREUSA
You didn't need to thop for the Cheezee-Q's®,
We already had dinner, and a snack.

ION
Kreon, is that you?

KREON
Ion?

ION
It is I. Ion.
Hello, my old Royal friend.

KREON
Hello to you too.
Honey, this is Ion.

ION
The Prophet Tiresias found me as a baby.

CREUSA
I hate to break up this moving reunion but can we hear the
   prophet or what?

ION
We're expecting some important clients,
So you may have to wait until the next available slot.

CREUSA
Honey, did you forget to make an appointment, honey?

KREON
No, honey, I made an appointment.

ION
Kreon, I'm afraid you didn't,
The only consultation today is for Creusa, the Queen of
    the Isthmus.

CREUSA
Oh, present.

ION
Oh, sorry, Creusa, ma'am,
Forgive me for not recognizing you as a Queen, you just
    look so young.

CREUSA
We Seven Sisters age halftime.

KREON
She does wear the Royal Ring of Two Pearls, look.

ION
Tiresias and I were taking a bus through Isthmus last year,
    we loved it!
I think it will flourish into a beautiful city.

CREUSA
Only if the prophet will quickly help Kreon with his
    reproductive problem,
And get us a son before my Seven Sister death.

KREON
Creusa's number is next.

(Lamb scream)

ION
That's the nocturne lamb being slaughtered in the bathtub.

KREON
Are you guys making shawarma?
I love shawarma.

ION
I'm sure swarma loves you too.
The intestines help Tiresias with her visions.

CREUSA
We better head in the Oracle Room while that bowel be hot.

KREON
I have to pee anyway.

(CREUSA removes her sandals. KREON almost enters the Oracle Room)

ION
Kreon! "No food, drink, or SHOES in the Oracle Room."

CREUSA
Why, honey, would you wear those tight, lace-up shoes?

KREON
I always wear them, honey.

CREUSA
But what about the rules, honey?

KREON
I didn't know the rules, honey.

CREUSA
You could have done some research, honey?

KREON
You're right, Creusa, I'm sorry.

CREUSA
No, I'm sorry, Kreon, I was mean, no excuse for it.

ION
Just remember the most important rule, "No violence."

CREUSA
Kreon is not a violent man,
Kreon is a very practical man,
Very practical man.
I'll be in there, honey.

(CREUSA exits. KREON unlaces his shoes)

ION
If you don't mind me saying, Kreon,
The way Creusa said "practical" made it seem like an insult.

KREON
That's interesting, Ion, because she meant it to be insulting.
Creusa asked me to marry her to merge some of my royal
  blood of Thebes with hers.
But she didn't even know me.
I think when she got to know me, she didn't like me.

ION
Oh come on Kreon, you're mostly likable.

KREON
Thanks.
Where's your stewpot?

ION
Tiresias asked me to remove it, said I was too old for it.

KREON
I have to admit, I'm excited to see Tiresias.
Apologize for what went down last year.

ION
She doesn't blame you for being blinded.
She's always been partial to you Kreon.

KREON
That's sweet.
Well, shoes are off, I should go join my Former-Queen.

ION
What do you mean Former-Queen?

KREON
Creusa has no more power.
The Isthmus population elected to be folded into the
  Democratic States of Athens.
But Creusa's convinced the Isthmus will trust her again
  once we have an heir.
But she swears my gene gel isn't exactly sticky,
If you know what I mean.

ION
I don't.

KREON
Well, Creusa can bear children.
While younger she was wondering Red Mountain and
  encountered Jason,
Living like a hermit in the overturned hull of the Argo.
In innocent romantic hope, she gave over to his seduction.
He shunned her and told her never to return.
Creusa secretly birthed their son, and through shame, she
  left that baby to die.

ION
That poor baby.

KREON
Creusa couldn't see any other action, being so young herself.
My wife has lived life haunted by that choice.
I think having a child now is redemption for her.
She's determined to become a mother, at any cost.

(Enter CREUSA)

CREUSA
Tiresias invited you to confer with her alone, Kreon.

KREON
Me? Alone? Por qua?

CREUSA
Didn't you two date?

KREON
Yes, but I don't think it could be about that.

CREUSA
Well, go find out.

(KREON awkwardly kisses CREUSA then exits into the Oracle Room. ION points the fan at CREUSA)

ION
May I ask Creusa, Seven Sister,
Does being royalty feel different than being like common
  people?

CREUSA
I don't know, I've never been like common people.

ION
It's just that I've always sensed that I'm of special birth.
Not better than others,
Just like maybe I'm destined to rule a land, somewhere.

CREUSA
I think many average children dream about being important.

(KREON enters and hugs ION)

KREON
Oh let me kiss you, Ion!
This is so crazy.

ION
You must have been bit by funny fleas, Kreon.

KREON
Oh, I'm so fond of you Ion.
When I say to Tiresias, "How can I hold a son?"
Tiresias says to me, "Go outside, embrace Ion."

ION
Wait wait wait. What?

KREON
I'm your father and you're my son.
"Embrace Ion, and you shall embrace someone to call son."

CREUSA
Then do you and I have a child later?

KREON
Unfortunately no, sorry. Tiresias swore no child would be
our issue.

(CREUSA exits into the Oracle Room)

ION
Really, I'm your son?

KREON
Does Tiresias lie?

ION
She does not.

KREON
Then, you're my son, Ion.

ION
Did you listen to that Cadmusaurus,
We have a Father!
And, and, aaaand you can rename me,
I was never partial to Ion.

KREON
Ion is a great name.
Because you keep your Eye-On the prize.

ION
I love prizes!
I am Ion!
Keeping my Eye-On the prize!
Oo! I just realized!
Someday I'll be the King of the Isthmus.
Oo! Oo!

KREON
Ion, settle down, I'm sorry, the Isthmus is under Theseus'
    control,
You won't be king.

ION
What will I be then?

KREON
If Isthmus royalty were a band,
You'll be like a back-up singer.

ION
Not quite as great as I dreamed,
But that was vanity, Kreon, or I should say now, Daddie.
Wait, Creusa will probably hate me.

KREON
Probably, she gets pretty angry.
Maybe later attempt friendship with her,
The strongest bonds are fashioned when the greatest fires cool.

(CREUSA enters)

CREUSA
Well hear-hear, we will commemorate, right?
I've inherited an heir to my throne, maybe get my population off my back.

KREON
You're accepting my son as your own?

CREUSA
How I could I deny him?
Do you have anything to drink, my new stepson?

ION
Creusa, stepmother, I do got drinks,
Some juice and many a mug featuring the most lovely animals.

(Exit ION)

KREON
Are you okay, Creusa?

CREUSA
Worry not for me, husband, bold bold courage has flown in through my window.

(CREUSA devilishly laughs. ODD-JOBS sing)

   [THE SONG OF NECESSARY DEFILEMENT]

(Enter ION carrying juice-filled coffee mugs in his stewpot)

ION
Tiresias put some mugs o'juice, in my stewpot.

CREUSA
In order to revel with grandeur,
Let me drop the two pearls from my ring in both your drink.

KREON
Not your mother's stunning Two-Pearl Ring.

CREUSA
Why have we great property if not to greatly enjoy it?
One pearl here. One here.

(CREUSA drops a pearl in each of the two mugs)

ION
To the future.

CREUSA
However long that be.

KREON
Wait wait, Ion, let me have your mug.
That rhino is great.

ION
This rhino mug is my favorite.

KREON
Son, obey your father.

(ION and KREON laugh as they exchange mugs)

KREON
Cheers.

(ALL drink. Silence)

ION
This juice is fortifying.

KREON
Hm, mine tastes funny.

CREUSA
Funny how?

(KREON gives his mug to CREUSA)

KREON
Like it's got some shrimp... Oh. The mug, 'tis poisoned.

(KREON starts convulsing)

CREUSA
Horrible deluded man!
I will not be a matron-head to adulterated buck ill-begotten
   by a diabolical bumble-boy.
I revolt, for you are revolting.
I take from you that which you have taken from me, hope
   for the future.

KREON
You could have just waited,
Sadnesses pass.

(KREON collapses)

ION
But why do I feel endowed with twice the verve, vigor and
   bravado?

CREUSA
Only one pearl from my mother be tainted,
While the other give great vitality,
I left it to fate to judge who would die.
Now in the death of your father, you, Ion,
Return to your common menial nothing life,
Your claim on nobility ends before it begins.

ION
So I'll end your life, Princess of Pain, in this holy studio
  apartment.
This seems my destiny, and I am charged by the might of
  your pearl to fulfill!

(ION horribly beats CREUSA with his stewpot)

ION
The desire for greatness is unholy.
Poets sing shamelessly about the glories of the great,
But much evil and pain comes with ambition.
But still we all want to be great, why?

(Just as ION is about to kill CREUSA with the stewpot,
TIRESIAS enters)

TIRESIAS
Hold, Ion, hold, end not Creusa's life,
Lest you will be tormented by the Furies, the hunters of
  Matricides.

CREUSA
(Near death) This stewpot, this ancient ark.
How did you come by it?

ION
It's the stewpot in which Tiresias found me as a baby.

CREUSA
When you were fresh born,
I abandoned you in that stewpot to die.
Ion, you're my son!

ION
Heh?

TIRESIAS
It's true, Ion, you're the son of this Seven Sister Queen,
  Creusa. As you sensed, you have royal blood.

ION
But why tell Kreon I was his son?

TIRESIAS
The full truth was not revealed until now, I saw that he
 would call you son, which is true.

ION
But now he's dead.

CREUSA
(*Near death*) From your giraffe-cup, pour forth juice down
 his throat,
The other pearl shall revive.

ION
But I should use the booster pearl for you, mother.

CREUSA
No son, it's time for my number to fall,
Give the juice to Kreon, go on.

ION
Drink fake father, drink.

(*ION pours the juice into KREON*)

CREUSA
I have a son, all these years, I had a son,
To see my Hæmon.

ION
Your which?

CREUSA
Before I tucked you in that stewpot to be taken by the toxic
 soil of the world,
I named you Hæmon.

ION
Hæmon, I knew that my name wasn't Ion, somehow.
I think from hence on hence, I shall be called Hæmon.

(An ODD-JOB changes ION's name to HÆMON)

CREUSA
Hæmon, my son, you were born into greatness.
Knowing that I could have killed you,
I should not live past the minute I acted toward malicious
  murder,
So son, lament not my suicide.
From this leap from life shall hope endure,
Let cynicism fall like Seven Sister Four.

(CREUSA runs into the bathroom. HÆMON follows her)

HÆMON
Mom, no.

TIRESIAS
Falling to the earth is the course of every life.

*(HÆMON enters with CREUSA's umbrella. An ODD-JOB
crosses off CREUSA and tallies her death)*

HÆMON
Creusa, leapt from the window to her death,
I couldn't save her.
I feel so strange.

TIRESIAS
As do all children upon waking from the dream of childhood.
And sadly, we must abandon this Apartment Temple.
You befouled her with violence, Ion.

HÆMON
I was defending Kreon.

TIRESIAS
The reason, or degree of righteousness, matters none, the
    action was done.
We must lock the doors to all who seek oracles and separate.
But know, you served me well.

HÆMON
Until the moment I didn't, then that one cruelty ruined all
    things good I had done.

TIRESIAS
Such is life, each second spent on selfish actions equals a
minute spent on the good.

HÆMON
Okay, thank you.

TIRESIAS
Good bye sir, and his tortoise.

HÆMON
Now hug me, please lady?

TIRESIAS
No, if I do, I will cry,
Tears cause too much pain to my ruined eyes.
I lose today everything worth my happiness.

HÆMON
That's a terrible thought to live with.

(KREON wakes up)

TIRESIAS
Hello, Kreon.

KREON
Oh, hello, sunshine.

TIRESIAS
Kreon, mind yourself, good-bye.

(Exit TIRESIAS)

KREON
Bye? What went on?

HÆMON
Kreon, Creusa leapt to her death,
Her Seven Sister number fell as an answer to her murder
of you.

KREON
But I live, son.

HÆMON
You do, Kreon, luckily.
But Creusa tried to kill you then she felt remorse and
welcomed her death,
Upon realizing I'm the son she abandoned to die.

KREON
That is some sad coincidence.

HÆMON
I think that too.

KREON
So, you're not my son?

HÆMON
Nope.

KREON
Fate is neither kind nor cruel.

HÆMON
You should write poems.

(HÆMON packs up the fans and puts them offstage)

KREON
I should entomb Creusa with the other fallen Seven Sisters,
The dust of the past cannot settle without a burial.

HÆMON
Kreon, Tiresias just left me,
Maybe, if you even for a second were excited to have me
    as a son,
Could my baby dragon and I stay with you?

KREON
I would like that,
I should have never deserted you and Tiresias.

HÆMON
This is good news.
Oh by the way, Creusa named me Hæmon.

KREON
Hæmon?

HÆMON
You know what Kreon,
It's hard to think the future will be better than the past
But I actually think it may.
And I get to hang out with Antigone some more.

(HÆMON, with his tortoise, and KREON exit)

ODD-JOB SOAPY
One year later, 47:
Œdipus.

*(Enter ŒDIPUS, ANTIGONE and JOKASTA carrying a
bottle of bleach and wearing the ruling Coat of Thebes)*

ŒDIPUS
Jokasta, honey, Thebes is falling apart, people are on the
    verge of rebellion,
You have to make some political decisions here.

JOKASTA
Bleach will fix everything.

(Enter THÍBA covered with her umbrella)

THÍBA
Rin-a-ring, Royal-in-laws.

ANTIGONE
Thíba.

JOKASTA
Stepma, you look terrible.

THÍBA
It's how I feel too.
But I just come from a convocation of the Bacchae.
They are done with your rule, Queen,
The Foxes demand complete abdication of the Coat.

JOKASTA
Who would I give the Coat to?

THÍBA
Me, Queen Jokasta, this has always been my city,
I can keep the Bacchae calm.

JOKASTA
You? Never!
Money grubber.

THÍBA
Excuse me.

ŒDIPUS
Thíba, please if you have sway over the Bacchae, calm them.

ANTIGONE
We have some new initiatives toward curing the Green
   Plague.

ŒDIPUS
Along the same lines as how I solved the riddle of the
   Hellbitch.

THÍBA
That was amazing, Œdipus.

(KREON enters with a bleeding head)

KREON
I just got pelted with a snow globe,
Why throw a snow globe?

JOKASTA
The best thing to do is to let this rebellion run its course.
Like I try to tell Œdipus, too much action causes too much
   friction.

KREON
That is one of the worst leadership strategies I have heard.

ANTIGONE
You should put some peroxide on that cut, Uncle.

JOKASTA
Or bleach, put some bleach on it.

ŒDIPUS
Thíba, if Jokasta gave the Coat to her brother would that
   calm the Bacchae?

THÍBA
  Maybe, for a spell.

KREON
Don't give me that wearable problem.

(Exit KREON)

ŒDIPUS
Just tell me anything,
Anything that will let me save Thebes.

THÍBA
I made Thebes flourish, let me be the Queen again.

JOKASTA
Never, Grubby!

THÍBA
Excuse me.

ANTIGONE
Mother, perchance you could give the Coat to Father.

JOKASTA
You want it?

ŒDIPUS
Yes!

JOKASTA
Fine, take it.

(JOKASTA takes off the Coat of Thebes, she has on boxer shorts and a t-shirt)

JOKASTA
I feel practically naked without the coat.

ANTIGONE
Because you are practically naked.

ŒDIPUS
Go get some clothes on.

JOKASTA
What will you do?

ŒDIPUS
Cure the Green plague.
I love you, Jokasta.

JOKASTA
I love you, Œdipoo.
(To THÍBA) Grubby.

(JOKASTA kisses ŒDIPUS then exits)

ŒDIPUS
Thíba, tell the Bacchae things will change.

THÍBA
You probably have a day, Œdipus, before it happens all over
    again.

*(THÍBA exits. ŒDIPUS has great frustration putting on the
Coat)*

ŒDIPUS
Where are the arm holes in this thing?
Arrr! You're a coat! A coat!

(ŒDIPUS starts slamming the Coat on the ground)

ANTIGONE
It's alright father, I'll help you.

ŒDIPUS
Thank you Antigone, I guess I looked pretty stupid.

ANTIGONE
A little, but I wouldn't worry about it, I'm the only one that
    saw you.

ŒDIPUS
Can you believe it, I feel so useless,
And I'm the man who solved the riddle of the Hellbitch.

ANTIGONE
I believe in you, Father.

(JOKASTA enters dressed)

JOKASTA
Antigone, go make sure the Twins get their breakfast.

ANTIGONE
They're teenagers, they don't need help eating anymore.
And it's almost dinner time.

JOKASTA
Just get out here okay.

ANTIGONE
Yes, ma'am.

(ANTIGONE exits)

JOKASTA
You spoil her.

ŒDIPUS *(flirty)*
I'll spoil you.

(Enter KREON)

KREON
Well, would you look at that, King Œdipus.

ŒDIPUS
By the end of the day, some things will actually change.

(Enter a filthy TIRESIAS)

TIRESIAS
Royal Family, ding-dong.

KREON
Infected lady, you cannot here.

TIRESIAS
Calm down, cheesy hands, I'm not afflicted with the
    Greeban Plague,
You had people searching all over for me.
{It's Tiresias.}
Ta-da!

KREON
Oh Tiresias, wow, you've changed a lot since I saw you last
  year.

JOKASTA
Why is she here?

KREON
Don't be mad sister, Œdipus and I had Tiresias tracked down.

ŒDIPUS
To see if she saw any answers.

TIRESIAS
I feel so welcome.

KREON
How have you been, Tiresias?

TIRESIAS
Muh, I just wander around talking to myself since Ion
defiled my Apartment Temple.
Now tell me why I was called back to Thebes.

ŒDIPUS
I want to cure the Green Plague.

JOKASTA
Look at me, look at my eyes.
Any story this seer spins is spleen, Œdipus.

TIRESIAS
Here's some spleen.
The one who seeks shall find, the one who seeks is blind.
To want to know what you do not want to know.
You need to strike out the pollution that pollutes your mind,
For you safely harbor the pathogen that feeds on your kind.

ŒDIPUS
What does that mean?

TIRESIAS
Bleed blood for blood bled,
For this infected blood bloodies your bloody people.

ŒDIPUS
What does that mean?

TIRESIAS
A person is the key to everything you don't know.
And fun fact, the first thing you don't know, this key killed
  Jokasta's husband.
The other one, not you.

JOKASTA
Ridiculous, a group of bandits killed my former husband,
In the days of the Hellbitch.

ŒDIPUS
I solved the Riddle of the Hellbitch.

KREON
That was fantastic.

TIRESIAS
Ah yes, the great solving of the Riddle of the Hellbitch,
By the great Œdipus, what an amazing beginning.

ŒDIPUS
It did begin my relationship with Thebes.

TIRESIAS
No, it began the end of your relationship with Thebes.

ŒDIPUS
I don't understand your riddles, Tiresias.
Everything in Thebes must help or be hurled.
I need answers, plain, plain answers.

TIRESIAS
How plain does wisdom need to be for one to plainly see
  what one does not to see?

ŒDIPUS
Okay, just tell me what to do, lady.

TIRESIAS
Walk away from Thebes, wander the Maddening
Wasteland, die on foreign ground.
Answer your own riddle.
Then give the Coat to Kreon.

KREON
Me? Why me?

TIRESIAS
Because there's no one else around.

ŒDIPUS
But there's me.

TIRESIAS
Is there?

JOKASTA
And me.

TIRESIAS
Really?

ŒDIPUS
We just need to cure the Green Plague.

TIRESIAS
Very well, ask me how.

ŒDIPUS
Okay, how can I cure the Green Plague?

TIRESIAS
You can't.
Next question.

ŒDIPUS
Don't you play with me, lady, you need to tell me the truth.

TIRESIAS
If I spoke the truth, you would soon ask me not to speak,
So heed the warning of your future self and ask me not for
the truth.

ŒDIPUS
My future self? I want the truth!
And I have no shame in ripping it from your head.

TIRESIAS
No one can make facts fall from another's mind.

ŒDIPUS
We'll see if that's true.
Tell me what you see!

(ŒDIPUS pushes his thumbs through the empty eyes of screaming TIRESIAS)

KREON
Œdipus, back off, are you trying to blind her again?

ŒDIPUS
If it can be done, I will do it.

TIRESIAS
Alright, alright, tell me, Œdipus, what doesn't lie?

ŒDIPUS
An honest man.

TIRESIAS
What object Œdipus, what object doesn't lie?

ŒDIPUS
A mirror.

TIRESIAS
Get a mirror and I'll show you something cool.

ŒDIPUS
Jokasta, give me a mirror.

JOKASTA
I just don't carry around mirrors.
But look into my eyes, they'll reflect what I see, baby.

TIRESIAS
Did you call him baby?
That's funny.
Because you…
And…
You'll get it later.
Œdipus, look into the mirror, what do you see?

ŒDIPUS
I see a compassionate ruler man,
I see the person that will cure the Green Plague.

TIRESIAS
Yes, you see the key to your questions.

ŒDIPUS
No, I see me.

TIRESIAS
Exactly.

KREON
Are you saying Œdipus is somehow connected to the
troubles of Thebes?

TIRESIAS
I'm not saying anything,
Are YOU saying Œdipus is connected to the troubles of
Thebes?

KREON
That seems to be what YOU are saying.

TIRESIAS
That seems to be what YOU are saying.

ŒDIPUS
Would you two stop, just stop your jib-jab,
I see it all now, old melodies don't quite fade from memory.

KREON
What?

ŒDIPUS
Kreon plays the records and Tiresias dances the dance.

KREON
What?

ŒDIPUS
You called Tiresias here because you're trying to steal the
Coat of Thebes,
Then you two can hook up again,
And rule together.

TIRESIAS
Œdipus, foolish man with wasted sight,
See what you be,
Blind judging blind,
And condemned judging free.

ŒDIPUS
Leave me auspex of un-terminated night,
You're no master of me,
Or anyone who feels the sun.

TIRESIAS
I never wanted to be here in the first place.
This city is violent, overpopulated, underfed, filled with plague,
And the air smells like Médée's rotten dragon.
Œdipus, see me, the Blind Seer, then later, in a day or so,
tell me who's the blind one.

KREON
Do you need something for your eyes?

TIRESIAS
Thebes has done enough for my eyes!

(Exit TIRESIAS)

JOKASTA
Œdipus, my brother would not conspire against you.

ŒDIPUS
Yes, he would, and he can follow his blind date out.
Hit the gates, bub.

KREON
Am I like, banished? Again?

ŒDIPUS
Help or be hurled.
Once more Thebes is done with you and you with her.

KREON
I didn't scheme against you.
Why would I want to rule?
I get all the benefits of royalty without the weight,
What man in his right mind would want more work for less
reward.

JOKASTA
Œdipus, you blame Kreon for bile spread by that vile seer.

ŒDIPUS
Jokasta, you're unseeing to your brother's ambitions.

KREON
Arguing with the self-righteous man is like begging the
dead to live.
If this is what you wish, my king, I'll be gone,
I'll wander the Wasteland, be subjected to Madness.

JOKASTA
Œdipus, look at me, look at my eyes.

Seers are hateful money-grubbers,
They report terrible things for payments,
Then out of fear, people make the predictions come true.
Too much action causes too much friction.
When I was young, newly married to my first husband,
For whimsy we went to visit a prophet.
Her visions portended horrible things about my first born son,
Including that he alone would murder his father.
So out of fear, my first baby-boy was ripped from my arms
   and killed.
When my husband met death it was by a group of bandits,
During the Onslaught at Three Road-Cross.
It was not the work of a single assailant.
Then you arrived and answered the Riddle of the Hellbitch.

KREON
Which was great.

JOKASTA
And we fell in love.
So my pretty boy, prophets foretell foolish prophesies.
Kreon is not trying to unseat you.

KREON
I'm good at obeying rules, not making them.

ŒDIPUS
Jokasta, did you say the Onslaught at Three Road-Cross?

JOKASTA
Yes.

ŒDIPUS
Tell me what your husband looked like.

JOKASTA
Strong chin, fantastic hair, a little like you.
I guess I have a type.

KREON
You do, you do.

ŒDIPUS
Several bandits killed him?

JOKASTA
There was too much carnage to be one man's work.

ŒDIPUS
How many other men died during this attack?

JOKASTA
There were four others that were slain.

ŒDIPUS
So five, five men were killed during the Onslaught at Three
   Road-Cross?

JOKASTA
Yes.

ŒDIPUS
Oh, sweetie, if you could listen up, that'd be great.
I was raised well-loved but I became so frightened by a
   prediction.
I ran, I ran so far away, not knowing where I was running.
I came upon Three Road-Cross, sure enough.
And I stalled not knowing where to go, panting, panicked.
A vehicle came up, five men total.
The driver yelled at me to move and hit me with a tire-iron.
So, without thinking I grabbed the black bar,
And struck him so hard, his head parted
like a pod bursting a pink flower.
Three others charged at me, I fought them off.
I acted so quickly, striking and striking,
Not thinking at all, exhausted from running, scared of the
   prophesy.
At last, the old man in the back of the vehicle, with a

weapon came at me.
And I struck and struck,
And the old man bled his golden blood.

JOKASTA
Œdipus, look at me, look at my eyes,
What was this prophecy you received?

ŒDIPUS
That I would dirty my mother's bed with my loathsome
  seed,
And kill the man that fathered me.

JOKASTA
That's strange,
Because that prophesy is the mirror of mine.

(The ODD-JOBS sing)

[THE MUSIC OF PERIPETEIA]

KREON
Œdipus, let me see your feet.

ŒDIPUS
Why?

KREON
Show me your feet.

JOKASTA
Don't do it husband.
Kreon weren't you just banished?

KREON
Please Œdipus, if you ever trusted me,
Show me your feet.
In your feet there are answers.

ŒDIPUS
I want answers.

(ŒDIPUS starts to remove his shoes)

JOKASTA
Kreon don't do this.

KREON
I'm only doing what was already done.

(ŒDIPUS shows his foot)

ŒDIPUS
Here is my foot.

KREON
Do you know where you got that scar?

ŒDIPUS
No.

KREON
Jokasta, tell him.

ŒDIPUS
How does Jokasta know?

JOKASTA
I don't.

KREON
Œdipus, while you were a baby, this woman nailed you to a
  tree through your feet.
Fearing a prophecy enough to do this cruelty,
But not enough to end the task.

ŒDIPUS
Jokasta, how did you come by me as a baby?

JOKASTA
I didn't, I didn't.

KREON
Œdipus, brace yourself,
Because we wretched creatures see wretched things.

ŒDIPUS
What?

JOKASTA
Kreon, shut up!

KREON
Sister, how can anyone stop the truth from being true?

ŒDIPUS
What's true?

JOKASTA
Too much action causes too much friction.
Gone is one husband and my newborn baby,
No more loss can I handle.

KREON
Jokasta gave birth to you.

ŒDIPUS
Gave birth to me?
What do you mean?

JOKASTA
Seek no more, unless you seek to ruin us.

KREON
If you're ruined, you've always been ruined.

ŒDIPUS
What?
What is going on?

JOKASTA
Nothing baby,
Nothing, nothing, nothing, nothing.

(JOKASTA kisses ŒDIPUS many times all over his face)

KREON
Œdipus, the prediction that was given to you,
The one from which you ran...

ŒDIPUS
I hope it never comes true.

KREON
It's too late,
It has come true.

JOKASTA *(singing)*
Ring-a-ring my baby,
Pocket full of maybe.

ŒDIPUS
That I would kill my father?
And sleep with my mother?

KREON
Yes.

ŒDIPUS
It's come true?

KREON
Yes.

ŒDIPUS
When?

KREON
Now!

JOKASTA
(Singing) Action, action,
We all fall down.

(ŒDIPUS finally realizes then vomits)

ŒDIPUS
Fortune has blessed me for so long,
But who has fortune been blessing?

KREON
I don't know.

ŒDIPUS
Not me but another.
Who wore my skin,
Kissed my friends,
Ate my food,
Another that owned my thoughts more than I, right?

KREON
I don't know.

ŒDIPUS
I'm not he,
But he is I.
And who is he,
And who am I,
Who am I?

KREON
I don't know.

JOKASTA
You see, I was a child, and I had a child,
I was told the pitiless destructive course of its life,
The wave of mutilation it would cause,
I was told to ruin him, erase him.
But I always saw my baby, I could never see the beast,
I smelt his clean skin, heard his crying pain,
Ruining such purity is against a mother's nature.
My baby was so cute, so cute,
My baby still is.

(JOKASTA goes to kiss ŒDIPUS)

ŒDIPUS
Don't.

JOKASTA
Just one more kiss, baby.

ŒDIPUS
Don't be sick.

JOKASTA
Œdipus, look at me, look at my eyes.

ŒDIPUS
Look at your eyes? Your eyes?
See you, my eyes, these eyes are your eyes, see?
These eyes, eyes, eyes, now no more to see what eyes do know.
These sights of woe, that eyes do know.
Drown me in darkness, eyes,
To know no more, eyes,
To see no more, eyes,
What cruel life has in store!
Eyes, eyes, no more, no more, no more!
Eyes!

(ŒDIPUS rips out his eyes, screaming)

ŒDIPUS
Now, see you your eyes.

(KREON tends to ŒDIPUS by putting his tie around his eyes. ŒDIPUS drops his bloody orbs, JOKASTA picks up, washes each with bleach, then kisses them)

JOKASTA
One clean kiss for my husband, one clean kiss for my son,
Then let all my clean kisses be silent done.

(JOKASTA drinks the bottle of bleach. KREON rushes to her)

KREON
No, Sister.

JOKASTA
I'm healthy, for the first time in thirty-five years,
I can finally breathe.

(JOKASTA convulses and dies. An ODD-JOB crosses out her name and tallies her death)

ŒDIPUS
Did Jokasta leave?

KREON
Yes, in a sense Œdipus, our queen is dead.
Let these woes wash over us as the tides do the earth.

(Enter THÍBA)

THÍBA
Oh, Œdipus.

KREON
Keep distance, Thíba.

ŒDIPUS
No, come on in and look upon what cannot look.

(Enter HÆMON, cradling his pet tortoise, followed by ANTIGONE and the twins, POLYNIKES and ETEOKLES)

POLYNIKES
What a foul mess.

ANTIGONE
Father, you poor man.

ŒDIPUS
Don't pity me, children.

ETEOKLES
How could we not, Father?

ŒDIPUS
Antigone, Polynikes, Eteokles,

Jokasta is gone, my mother is gone,
Your double mother is gone,
The teeming womb that bore me a twofold harvest is gone.

POLYNIKES
{Eteokles, is our father saying that our mother is his
mother too?}

ETEOKLES
{Brother, some things are best not to ponder.}

ŒDIPUS
Please, Antigone, take me to rest.

KREON
Œdipus, I am afraid rest is not possible for you,
Think on your covenant with the city,
To help or be hurled from the gates of Thebes.
The Maddening Wasteland calls for thee.

THÍBA
Please Kreon, after this day, let Œdipus sleep.

KREON
How can I, Thíba?
He is somehow the cause of our Green Plague,
Does not your city long to breathe clean air?

THÍBA
It does.

KREON
Then he must be gone.

THÍBA
So be it.

ANTIGONE
How can all of you believe Father is the cause of the illness?

KREON
As the last child of Cadmus I must guard this city,
I must grab any chance I can to help her people,
No matter how remarkable, fantastic, or unbelievable.
This is the meaning of being a citizen, all will always be
  more than one.
Years will show wisdom to this.

ANTIGONE
Why wish to be wise if wisdom causes woe?

KREON
Go ahead Antigone, act in ignorance, see how well you fare.

ANTIGONE
If ignorance allows compassion,
Then let me act as ignorant as an ass.

KREON
Oh, do asses act compassionately?

ANTIGONE
Asses act as asses do,
And if an ass can act, it acts like you.

ŒDIPUS
Antigone, mind yourself!

ANTIGONE
Yes, sir.

ŒDIPUS
Help or be hurled,
Kreon is right.

ANTIGONE
How can you take his side?

ŒDIPUS
Sides Antigone?

Life is not match fought over sides,
We mix together, and must suffer the occasional clash in
   the middle.
I must leave Thebes as her fallen King.
Kreon, take care of this city, the Coat is yours.

KREON
I would rather the Green Plague than that Coat,
Let it go to the twins.

ŒDIPUS
They are too young.

ETEOKLES
History has had many teenage rulers.

ŒDIPUS
Kreon will act as regent until the twins reach age.

ETEOKLES
Then which one of us gets to wear the Coat of Thebes?
ŒDIPUS
Exchange power annually, so neither becomes too mired in
   this foul mess.
May your rule be better blest than mine.

POLYNIKES
{How could it not?}

ŒDIPUS
I am banished from Thebes,
I am banished from the progress of humanity.
I am gone, I am sorry.
I solved the riddle of the Hellbitch.

KREON
I'm still impressed.

(The ODD-JOBS sing)

[THE SONG OF SICKNESS]

ŒDIPUS
No one cry, every man will have his day,
But every day must have its night.

(ŒDIPUS removes the Coat of Thebes, says good-bye to his family and exits)

HÆMON
Papa, please, Œdipus will go mad and die,
Blindly walking with no one through the Wasteland.

ANTIGONE
No he won't, I will go with him.
Make sure he survives,
Secure his sanity, be his only company.

KREON
If you want to, Antigone, I certainly won't stop you.

ANTIGONE
Bye Twins, I will miss you both.

POLYNIKES
We love you Antigone.

(POLYNIKES hugs ANTIGONE)

HÆMON
But, Antigone, the Wastcland will cause you both to go mad.

ANTIGONE
Oh, Hæmon, I'm already pretty mad.
Bye, Regent Kreon.

(ANTIGONE exits. HÆMON exits. KREON closes the sliding door)

KREON
Anyone else want to go?
Polynikes?

ETEOKLES
I'm Eteokles, Uncle.

KREON
I can't keep you twins straight.
Do you want to leave Thebes?

ETEOKLES
I love Thebes, City life suits me.

KREON
Polynikes?

POLYNIKES
I'm good, until I get to rule, Uncle,
When my twin and I will trade the Coat every year.

ETEOKLES
But if you're unhappy Kreon,
I could take the Coat of Thebes now.

KREON
We'll see, Polynikes.

ETEOKLES
I'm Eteokles.

KREON
Get your mother prepared for her funeral.
The dust of the past cannot settle,
Without a burial.

POLYNIKES
Come along, Mommy.

(POLYNIKES exits with dead JOKASTA. KREON grabs the Coat of Thebes)

KREON
King Kreon, sounds ridiculous.
This Coat feels ill.

(Exit KREON)

THÍBA
You seem more eager to rule, Eteokles, than Kreon.

ETEOKLES
Thíba, I am.
Please, tell the Bacchae when I'm king in a few years,
If any of them survive the Green Plague,
I want them in my cabinet, making decisions.
I'll even make you my viceroy if you want, Thíba.
I mean crap,
You can't be happy with the way Thebes will be chronicled
    now.
Then let's clean these streets for our legacy's sake, Seven Sister,
The Bacchae want freedom, darn it, so do I.
But in the meantime,
Let's make the best of the foul mess we got, Step-Grandma.

THÍBA
Deal, Eteokles.

(THÍBA holds out her hand to shake)

ETEOKLES
Don't touch me, you're all plague-y.

(Exit ETEOKLES and THÍBA, separately)

ODD-JOB ERDIE
So much happened, I need to eat to fill my brain holes.

ODD-JOB SOAPY
I'm not sure what those are, Erdie,
But there is food around.

ODD-JOB ALICE
Enjoy.
Fifteen minutes.
(The ODD-JOBS exit)

END OF
ALL OUR TRAGIC
ACT III

ACT IV

(The ODD-JOBS enter)

ODD-JOB ERDIE
I feel like it's flying by, Soapy.

ODD-JOB SOAPY
A little like life, Erdie.

ODD-JOB ALICE
Back to work,
And let's work hard,
And work well.

(The ODD-JOBS sing)

> *[THE SONG ABOUT ACT FOUR'S*
> *SEMBLANCE OF WONDER]*

ODD-JOB SOAPY
You sounded great, Erdie.

ODD-JOB ERDIE
Thank you.

ODD-JOB ALICE
Act 4 all takes place during a weekend in year 50.

ODD-JOB SOAPY
Friday: The Mausoleum.

(THESEUS enters wearing the Minotaur horns on his back and carrying flowers)

THESEUS
Hopefully, loved ones, you have tranquility.

(THESEUS lays the flowers down)

ANTIGONE *(screaming offstage)*
Wake up, city!
Waaaake up!
Heeeeeelp!
Help!
It's my father, heeeeelp.

(ANTIGONE opens the sliding door and enters, dragging ŒDIPUS by a rope tied to each of their waists)

THESEUS
Lift him up here.
(Helps sit ŒDIPUS upright)
What happened?

ANTIGONE
He collapsed this morning.
We spent three years traveling the Maddening Wasteland.

THESEUS
Three years? Are you sane?

ANTIGONE
Barely.
I can't say the same for my father.

THESEUS
What happened to his eyes?

ANTIGONE
He ripped them out,
This is the fallen king of Thebes, Œdipus.

THESEUS
Oh no.

(THESEUS retreats from ŒDIPUS)

ANTIGONE
What's your problem?

THESEUS
Œdipus can't stay here.
We just eliminated the last case of Theban Green Plague.

(ŒDIPUS jolts awake)

ŒDIPUS
Antigone!

ANTIGONE
Yeah.

ŒDIPUS
Where are we?
Do I smell flowers?

THESEUS
You're in sacred Mausoleum of Athens where all my family
    is entombed.

ŒDIPUS
Who are you? Who's this, please tell me.

ANTIGONE
Just another jerk standing in our way.

THESEUS
Theseus, King of Athens.

(ANTIGONE suddenly kneels)

ANTIGONE
Oh, noble Theseus, forgive me, I didn't recognize you,
Please allow my father to stay.

THESEUS
Five years ago, I attempted peace with Thebes,
And a woman got blinded.

ŒDIPUS
Please, one man to another man, one former king to a
    present one,
Just let me rest with your solemn loves.

ANTIGONE
What's the harm?
Everyone here is already dead.

THESEUS
I'll randomly poll seven of my citizens,
If five approve then Athens will allow it.

ANTIGONE
Five of the seven you say?
How about three?

THESEUS
Five.

ANTIGONE
Four?

THESEUS
Five.

ANTIGONE
Four.

THESEUS
Six.

ANTIGONE
Five.

THESEUS
Five.

ANTIGONE
Can't you just decide as King,
Whether your citizens agree or not.

THESEUS
Oh Antigone,
No.

(Exit THESEUS)

ŒDIPUS
Antigone, this Mausoleum will be a fitting place for you to
   let me die.

ANTIGONE
I won't let you die, father.

ŒDIPUS
Not let me die?
Next you'll be asking flowers to stop their course in bloom.
Is someone else here?

ANTIGONE
Only the dead.

(Enter KREON drinking some Dragon-Head Coffee®)

KREON
Whew, I found you, finally.
Antigone, you grew these three years.

ŒDIPUS
{Why is Kreon here?}

ANTIGONE
Not sure.

KREON
Antigone, everyday, Hæmon says how much he misses you.

ANTIGONE
Well don't let him miss you too, Kreon, return to Thebes.

KREON
Sorry niece, I'm not going back just yet.

ANTIGONE
What do you need from us?

KREON
Three years ago,
Eteokles ended my monthlong regency and claimed the
Coat for herself.
Now Thebes flourishes.
Eteokles is the glorious Empress of Thebes.
She granted the members of the Bacchae high-level
   government positions,
Viceroy Thíba is cured and initiating real reforms.
Médée's Dragon was exhumed and burnt at an orchestrated
   rally,
Then the sickness disappeared.
It turns out that decaying creature, of which we were all so
   proud,
Was the source of the Green Plague.

ŒDIPUS
I thought I was the cause of the Green Plague,
That's why you banished me.

KREON
We were wrong.
Now, Eteokles in honor of your return is naming you the
Honorary Father of Thebes.

ŒDIPUS
Antigone, what did Kreon just say?

ANTIGONE
I heard the words but I don't trust their meaning.

ŒDIPUS
All those years in the Wasteland,
Staving off madness, we waited for this dignity to revisit.

ANTIGONE
No, father, we slogged through sand, time, insanity with no
  ambition beyond survival.
Only pride will tempt your return.
If you seek life, comfort, love, I give you all.
If Thebes wants you back, it's not to give you a title.
We know this.
It's rotten.

KREON
Eteokles wants Œdipus to live exalted in Thebes,
She even planned a huge banquet.

ŒDIPUS
I'm getting a banquet?

KREON
All due to your daughter, Empress Eteokles.

ANTIGONE
Even if this were true,
It's too soon to dive back into the Wasteland.
Your health needs to improve, here, with me.
You can't be attending any banquets.

ŒDIPUS
Thebes needs Œdipus,
So Œdipus shall rise again,
He lives to be honored,
And is honored to live.

KREON
Oh noble Œdipus, your return shall make Thebes glorious.

(Enter POLYNIKES, riding a child's bike)

POLYNIKES
Kreon's going down.

KREON
Polynikes!

ANTIGONE
Brother, you better be here with good in your heart.

POLYNIKES
Nothing but good, nothing but good.
Now, give up a hug, sis.

(ANTIGONE hugs POLYNIKES)

ŒDIPUS
Is this my son?

POLYNIKES
Affirmly Old Man.

(POLYNIKES pops open a large can of an energy drink)

ŒDIPUS
What's that smell?

POLYNIKES
BetaMaxx®.
I love the boosts it gives.

KREON
An energy drink he's addicted to.

ANTIGONE
Did Eteokles send you to find us?

POLYNIKES
No way, Eteokles is a Golddigger, sitting on piles of coins,
Drinking fresh-fruit smoothies in historical outfits.

KREON
I warn you Antigone, listen not Polynikes.

POLYNIKES
No, listen yes to me.
Eteokles and I were supposed to exchange the Coat every year,
Like Pop wanted.
But after three years I was like, "My turn,"
Then Eteokles banished me from Thebes.
This dummy Kreon is helping her.

KREON
The truth is,
Not one citizen wants Polynikes to take the throne away
    from our Empress.
When Polynikes was scheduled to lord,
He was off with women of questionable convictions.
{He caught crabs.}

POLYNIKES
That's not true, I'm married, to a beautiful princess.

KREON
He's not married.

POLYNIKES
I'm so married, her name's Argea, here's a picture.

(POLYNIKES shows a picture)

KREON
He cut that picture out of a magazine.

POLYNIKES
Pop, help me set Thebes right.

ŒDIPUS
It sounds like Thebes is set right, by Eteokles.
She's giving me a banquet.

POLYNIKES
A banquet, what?

KREON
You see Œdipus, the only problem Thebes has,
Which is kind of a huge problem, is Polynikes,
Huge problem.

POLYNIKES
Is that a fat joke?

ANTIGONE
How is Polynikes a problem?

KREON
He vows to rip Eteokles off the throne.

POLYNIKES *(Excited)*
Yeah!

KREON
Or destroy Thebes.

POLYNIKES *(Ashamed)*
Ya.

ŒDIPUS
Polynikes, you're rebelling against Thebes?

POLYNIKES
In order to fight the axis of Eteokles, Thíba and Mr. Mean-
    jeans, Kreon,
I enlisted me a merry band of malcontents,
We call ourselves the .07,
In honor of us being the silenced minority!
We got a viral catch phrase, .07 Free!

KREON
Point-oh-seven reflects no real statistics,
He just made that number up.

POLYNIKES
Yes, uh, I mean, it's like, .07's a super catchy number.

KREON
He wanted to name his army the Foxes,
But he was threatened with copyright lawsuits from the
  Bacchae.

POLYNIKES
The Bacchae are so mainstream you would not believe it.
So we came up with the .07.

KREON
The .07 is as a mismatched motley army as e'er man
  assembled.
For the past two years, his "soldiers" wait outside the
  Theban gates,
While waiting for Polynikes to order the attack.
Tapping into our power supply, hijacking food trucks, and
  scaring away toruists.
Practicing more hootenannies than military training.

POLYNIKES
Judge not my joyousness!
I have the right to rule being eldest in the line of succession.

KREON
You and Eteokles are twins,
You're older by a a few minutes.

ŒDIPUS
Do any of the Theban people actually want me back?

POLYNIKES + KREON *(Lying)*
Yes.

POLYNIKES
You need to return and bless my throne Father.

KREON
What throne is that?
The one at the bonfire?

POLYNIKES
The Coat of Thebes is mine, I'm the eldest child.

KREON
Elder by a few minutes!

ŒDIPUS
Antigone, I want to be wanted.

ANTIGONE
Yeah, but you know you're not.

ŒDIPUS
Can I dream?

ANTIGONE
No, all dreams end in disappointment.

ŒDIPUS
You're right, like most of the time.
Kreon, Polynikes, I won't go with either of you.

KREON
Oh sad, I was hoping it wouldn't come to this.
Œdipus, by order of Empress Eteokles, I must drag you
  back to Thebes.

ŒDIPUS
Drag me?
To my banquet?

ANTIGONE
Over my corpse, Kreon, will you drag my father away.

KREON
That shouldn't be too difficult.

(KREON attempts to push ANTIGONE but POLYNIKES grabs KREON in a bear hug and shakes him)

POLYNIKES
Polynikes!

(Enter HÆMON, exhausted)

HÆMON
Hold on, hold on.

KREON
Hæmon, this is not your business.

HÆMON
You're right, because the business being conducted here is
  crooked.

ANTIGONE
And you'll straighten it, Hæmon?

HÆMON
I ran as fast as I could through the Wasteland tracking
  Polynikes from his war-camp.
He stole that little bike from a little kid.

POLYNIKES
I wasn't going to walk the whole way.
BetaMaxx®.

HÆMON
Antigone, I'm not sure how much exposition you need here,
But Tiresias talked to both Kreon and Polynikes with an
  oracle.

ANTIGONE
What prophesy?

KREON
Hæmon, share no more.

HÆMON
Antigone, I could only gather is that Œdipus has a
  "Significant Future."

ŒDIPUS
I have a "Significant Future?"
I felt it, I felt it.

HÆMON
And that your dead body is quite important.

ŒDIPUS
What do you mean my dead body?

KREON + POLYNIKES
{You should not have said that.}

ŒDIPUS
What about my body?
Will anyone answer me!

(Enter TIRESIAS)

TIRESIAS
I'll tell the great King what he wants to hear.
If I don't, he might stick his thumbs in my eye-holes again.

ŒDIPUS
Ah, my old friend, Tiresias.

TIRESIAS
Œdipus, I've come for your tragedy.

ŒDIPUS
But you saw my "Significant Future."

TIRESIAS
Oh yes, your future is very significant,

But you don't live through most of it.
In your blood is a corrosion that cannot be cured,
Death is on her way, coming fast and soon.

ŒDIPUS
I'm dying?

TIRESIAS
Aren't we all?

ŒDIPUS
And you wanted to make my momentary life a little more
   miserable,
By pitting my family against me.

TIRESIAS
You humiliated and abused me.

ŒDIPUS
Violence set loose is violence returned.

TIRESIAS
But it's not all downside for you, Blind King, you gain in
   death what was lost in life.

ŒDIPUS
What does that mean?

TIRESIAS
Your body be blessed, lost Child of Tossed Thebes,
Grateful is the land under which you lie.
You give hope, promise and advancement to the one that
   buries you.
First decide who gets your corpse.
Then, do the easy part of this prophecy.

ŒDIPUS
What's that?

TIRESIAS
You have to die.

ŒDIPUS
And in death, I gain salvation?

TIRESIAS
You could call it that.

ŒDIPUS
So Kreon, I'm not getting a banquet?

KREON
No, I'm sorry old friend.
Eteokles, our Empress, sent me to claim your body to bury
you in Thebes.

ŒDIPUS
And Polynikes, you just want my corpse as a symbol?

POLYNIKES
More like a token, Father Brother, to be exchanged for
victory against Eteokles.

ŒDIPUS *(laughing)*
I feel so stupid,
I felt needed.
I'm sorry I ever doubted you, Antigone.

ANTIGONE
Don't think on it again, sir.

ŒDIPUS
And Tiresias, I regret my cruelty toward you.

TIRESIAS
Good, Blind King, a life lived without guilt is a life lived
without improvement.
But if it makes you feel any better I, like you, die
underappreciated and underground.

ŒDIPUS
It doesn't make me feel better.

TIRESIAS
Me neither, but now we know.
Hæmon, before I go, come over here and hug me?

HÆMON
Pleasurably, Tiresias..

TIRESIAS
Mind that tortoise, okay.

HÆMON
I will.
I love you.

TIRESIAS
Don't.
It's easier to pass through this life imagining I am unloved.
Bye-bye, Kreon.

KREON
Bye Tiresias.
Even with your manipulating me to get back at Œdipus,
It was still, as always, good seeing you.

TIRESIAS
I can't say it was good to see you,
Only because I have no eyes.

(TIRESIAS exits, passing THESEUS)

THESEUS
{Lots of blind inclusion today.}
Hi everyone, I'm Theseus.

(Everyone says awkward hellos)

THESEUS
Œdipus, I polled a group of my citizens,
They all say you may die in the Mausoleum of Athens.

ŒDIPUS
Thank you.

KREON
Theseus, where will the body of Œdipus settle?
The one that buries him gains fortune.

POLYNIKES
Theseus, hello, yes, over here, thank you.
Once Œdipus dies his body belongs to his eldest child, me.

ŒDIPUS
Can't I have a say in this?

KREON
Not by law, Œdipus.

THESEUS
Being in this Mausoleum, in Athens you're all subject to our laws,
We guarantee citizens can decide their own death rites.

ŒDIPUS
Then let me live out my brief life by those flowers.

THESEUS
You heard the man.

KREON
Theseus, will you deny Thebes her rightful claim?
That could be seen as a declaration of war.
You see, I bring the gilded voice of Thebes.

THESEUS
Do you want to bring Thebes to war with Athens?

KREON
Maybe Theseus, so grant Thebes her desire,
Or feel the fiery fist of justice wrap upon your door.

THESEUS
Right now, Kreon, you and your fiery fist shame me, you see.
You're shaming me, my city and yourself.

KREON
You would do this for a faithless father killer,
An incestuous reject?

THESEUS
This and more for any man that asks for help.

POLYNIKES
Thank you, fair Theseus, for giving me my father.

THESEUS
Œdipus, do you want to go with your son?

ŒDIPUS
I love him, but how can I choose what child I love best?
I want to be buried in this Mausoleum
And give Athens my body and blessing.

THESEUS
I'll go consult those citizens again,
See if we accept this gift of Œdipus.

(Exit THESEUS)

POLYNIKES
Brother, by staying here you beckon death for me.

ŒDIPUS
No son, you call it for yourself.

ANTIGONE
Polynikes, call off your .07,
Wise up, don't ruin yourself along with Thebes,
Keep moving forward,
Keep making connections.
Be a good husband for your new wife, Argea.
Start a family.

POLYNIKES
My wife's picture is from a magazine.
(Crumples the picture)
No woman would have me until I'm King of Thebes,
When I have the nobility promised by my birth.

ANTIGONE
Birth promises no one anything but a few beats of a heart
    too soon to be broken.
You want blood for blood's sake.
You and your twin will both die.

POLYNIKES
It's the choice of Eteokles,
She could give me the Theban Coat.

ANTIGONE
You could just walk away from this fight.

POLYNIKES
Walk away,
As I do now.
Look upon me, Antigone,
My lovely sister,
You shall not see your brother's face filled with life again.

ANTIGONE
I love you Polynikes, but you will lose, cause us all to lose.
Please don't leave me.

POLYNIKES
Don't cry for me Antigone,
The truth is...
I already left you.

(POLYNIKES crushes his BetaMaxx® can and bikes away)

ŒDIPUS
I can't fight any more,
I want to sleep.

KREON
That's wise Œdipus, no more fighting.

ANTIGONE
Why are you even still here, Kreon?

ŒDIPUS
Let him stay Antigone, after everything, Kreon, gives me comfort.

ANTIGONE
You remain a mystery to me.

(Enter THESEUS)

THESEUS
My citizens have spoken.
Athens shall accept your offering, King Œdipus,
Once death comes, I shall lay you to rest.

ANTIGONE
You promise to honor my father until he dies, Theseus?

THESEUS
A wasp is our word,
Honored oaths can take wing,
Disrespect what is sworn,
Then expect the sting.

ŒDIPUS
Theseus, I like your city, I think if I had followed your way of rule,
Letting the population guide me,
I would have had a better go at being king those twelve minutes.
Kreon, tell Thebes I'm glad it found its ideal ruler, I'm sorry it wasn't me.
And remind them, I solved the riddle of the Hellbitch.

KREON
It really was fantastic.

ŒDIPUS
Alright friends, you heard Tiresias,
I leave not this Mausoleum alive,
Let me sleep by those flowers until death comes,
As it comes for us all.

ANTIGONE
No Father, you're not dying,
The seer was being spiteful.

ŒDIPUS
Out of sweetness and spite, trust spite to have more truth.
Antigone, these past years have been an odd delay of
   death,
Just let me sleep.

ANTIGONE
There is no way while I live, sir, I will let you sleep.
Wait it out.

ŒDIPUS
Wait for what?
More pain, shame, self-soiling?

ANTIGONE
You're not thinking clearly,
I can help you heal.

ŒDIPUS
Daughter, violent acts I have done,
Horrific shows of horrific deeds I have enacted,
And I sought penance for my transgressions.
But how could one find forgiveness without actively doing
   wrong.
Yet, without doing, I have done wrong.

I want my last act to be a graceful gesture in and of itself,
Not a rebuttal to any offense done unto me,
Then I may leave this whole foul mess behind and perhaps
  find peace.
Good night Antigone. Good night Athens.
I am Œdipus of Thebes!
But now in death, I am yours!
This is best, I hope you'll recognize that.

(ŒDIPUS lays down, ANTIGONE sits him up)

ANTIGONE
Wait!
Father, please.

HÆMON
Antigone, come on, let your father rest.

ŒDIPUS
Listen to the him,
Now give me a last kiss good-bye.

(ANTIGONE kisses ŒDIPUS on his eyes)

ANTIGONE
One last kiss for my father,
One last kiss for my friend,
Let all my last kisses last till the end.

ŒDIPUS
Thank you, Princess Annie, for the wonder that is you.

ANTIGONE
No need to thank the one that receives the gift.

(ANTIGONE lays ŒDIPUS down. The ODD-JOBS sing)

   [THE FAREWELL SONG OF HOME]

*(ANTIGONE feels her father's pulse, arranges his body,
then unties the rope. The song ends)*

HÆMON
I hope I never have to see you die, Papa.

KREON
I wouldn't be able to live on if you died.

HÆMON
Maybe we can die at the same time.

THESEUS
Antigone, your father was proud of you.

ANTIGONE
And I was proud of him.

KREON
I'm sure, King Theseus, Ægeus would be proud of you,
Building such a model government.

THESEUS
That goat guy was proud of me if I could spell my name.

KREON
Come on Hæmon, back to Thebes,
I'm not looking forward to telling our Empress I failed.

HÆMON
Antigone, where are you off to now?

ANTIGONE
I'll return to Thebes, it's the soil in which I belong.

HÆMON
Then you'll keep us company through the Wasteland.

ANTIGONE
If you care to keep company with a broken heart.
But first I give my father a funeral,
The dust of the past cannot settle without a burial.

(ANTIGONE arranges her father's body)

HÆMON
Papa, Antigone seems mad at me for suggesting she let
   Œdipus sleep.

KREON
She probably is mad at you.

HÆMON
But wasn't I right, Œdipus wanted to end his suffering.

KREON
It doesn't matter if you were right or not,
A person doesn't like being shown she is wrong.

HÆMON
Good lesson, Papa.

(Exit KREON and HÆMON)

THESEUS
Antigone, you can stay in Athens, I could use your strength,
   your guidance,
Avoid the bloody civil-war about to begin in Thebes.

ANTIGONE
It's my bloody civil-war, Theseus,
I should watch my siblings die.
Come on, King, help me.

THESEUS
We can keep your father next to mine.

ANTIGONE
That's kind.

THESEUS
Do good Antigone, don't expect gold, gifts or glory,
Do good, for goodness sake, do good.

ANTIGONE
Is there another option?

(THESEUS and ANTIGONE exit with dead ŒDIPUS)

ODD-JOB ALICE
Still year 50, the next day,
Saturday: .07 Against Thebes.

(Rambunctiously, POLYNIKES, KAPANEÚS and TYDEUS—collectively called the .07—enter, like young rambunctious teenagers)

.07ERS
(Chanting) .07, .07, .07, .07 free!

POLYNIKES
Go Tydeus. Go Tydeus!

(TYDEUS does some free-styling, then the .07 clap)

POLYNIKES
.07 free!

(On the platform, enter KREON and HÆMON carrying his pet tortoise. KAPANEÚS sees them)

KAPANEÚS
May all Thebes get Green Plague!

KREON
Thank you, Kapaneús.

(KAPANEÚS throws a BetaMaxx® can at them)

TYDEUS
The Empress sucks.
.07!

POLYNIKES
.07 free!

(The .07 exits chanting)

HÆMON
Point zero-seven reflects the amount of decency they have.

KREON
Why wait two years, threatening attack, but doing nothing?

HÆMON
Action is filled with answers, waiting is filled with hope.
And without hope what are we?
Unpicked fruit left to rot in field.

KREON
That's nice,
Without hope, what are we?

(Enter ΦILOKTETES)

ΦILOKTETES
Are you King Kreon?

KREON
Yes, I mean I'm Kreon but not King.
I was regent but that ended as fast as it began.
This is my son Hæmon.

ΦILOKTETES
Merry Dragon Day, to you both.

KREON
Is it Dragon Day?

ΦILOKTETES
I think so, yes.

KREON
We haven't celebrated Dragon Day since my father
Cadmus deserted us.
What can I do for you?

ΦILOKTETES
Kreon, I am Φiloktetes, cousin to the Seven Sisters,
One of them being Creusa, who was briefly your wife.

HÆMON
Just in the nature of disclosure,
I'm Creusa's son, who under the influence of a pearl, beat
  her.
If you want to enact revenge now is a good time to
declare it.

ΦILOKTETES
I heard Creusa tried to murder the both of you before she
  leapt to her own demise.
So no revenge to be had.

HÆMON
Thank goodness,
I couldn't fight you,
You have the bow that belonged to Herakles.

ΦILOKTETES
The Palladium Bow yes,
You see, Herakles was my dearest friend,
In torment, he called for some one to ignite his funeral
  pyre,
None could burn him, except for me.
As a reward I received his Palladium Bow.

*(AGAMEMNON enters flanked by ODYSSA and MENELAUS,
all dressed as military)*

AGAMEMNON
Kreon, Theban Guard reporting on the threat-level.

KREON
Go ahead, Agamemnon.

AGAMEMNON
Once again the Point-O'Seven show no sign of attacking.

ΦILOKTETES
Captain Agamemnon, you're just the man I came to see.

AGAMEMNON
I am?

ΦILOKTETES
You're married to my Seven Sister cousin Klytaimnēstra.
I am Φiloktetes.

AGAMEMNON
Okay?

ODYSSA
Honored to meet the legendary companion of Herakles.
Odyssa.

MENELAUS
Menelaus.
I'm married to Seven Sister Helen with the prized looks.

ΦILOKTETES
Today is 30 A.H,
Thirty years to the day After Herakles,
Thirty years to the day,
That Herakles asked me to burn him alive.
These past three decades without him,
I feel abandoned, what is the world now?
What am I?
I thought with my military skill,
Having trained with my heroic friend,
I could be useful somewhere.
I hope to enlist under you to have the adventure of defending
    Thebes.

AGAMEMNON
I'm afraid I have all the soldiers I need.

ΦILOKTETES
Please, I'll do anything.

ODYSSA *(in private)*
{Agamemnon, having access to the Palladium Bow would
  be foolish to deny.}

AGAMEMNON
Uck, Φiloktetes, let's go.
We definitely will not need that strange wig.

ΦILOKTETES
It's a hat, sir, my lucky fur-cap.

*(Exit ΦILOKTETES, AGAMEMNON, ODYSSA and
MENELAUS. Enter ANTIGONE with a toolbox)*

ANTIGONE
Kreon, Hæmon.

KREON
Eteokles had me call Tiresias for some counseling,
I'll see if she arrived.

(Exit KREON)

HÆMON
How did the memorial for you father turn out?

ANTIGONE
I got more nails in my fingers than in the wood.

HÆMON
By the way, Cadmusaurus thinks you look great.

ANTIGONE
Well your turtle is lying,
Because I obviously don't.

HÆMON
"No, you turtle-ly look great."
But all puns aside, he's a baby dragon.

ANTIGONE
Do you need something from me, Hæmon, or can I take a
   shower?

HÆMON
Every second I'm not by you, I miss you,
There it is. Said.
I know you're upset about your dad,
But I traveled through the Maddening Wasteland with
Cadmusaurus to help you.
Know, here is someone who cares.
Right here, see this guy, this guy cares.
And his baby dragon would too if it weren't cold-blooded.
So, listen to me!
...I'm not good at being assertive, so please, listen, if you
   don't mind.
I know these are not days meant for love, Antigone.
Last night, when we returned from Athens,
I went to talk with Polynikes, I needed his permission as
your male elder now.

ANTIGONE
Male elder?

HÆMON
Antigone, long have I loved you,
Long have I longed to be by your side,
Though I often annoy you, I know how you feel about me.

ANTIGONE
Like a wounded bird,
How could anyone hate a wounded bird?
No matter how much he pecks at your hands.

HÆMON
That was mean,
But you can't change what's in the heart.

I will always stay true.
Antigone, behold, my hand,
Join you your hand to mine.

ANTIGONE
Like hold your hand?

HÆMON
No, marry me.

ANTIGONE
What, no,
You're crazy.

HÆMON
Crazy for you.
I have loved you since we were kids,
When I was called Ion.
{You know, I'm the same kid, right?}

ANTIGONE
Hæmon, if you were any cuter I would smother you.
But what you need to do now is give me time, okay?
My father just died,
I just discovered the Twins want to murder each other,
You see, I'm not used to… people.

HÆMON
Okay, Antigone, I understand.
I'm sorry. I should have been more sensitive.

(ANTIGONE kisses HÆMON then exits. POLYNIKES enters and scares HÆMON)

POLYNIKES
.07 free!

HÆMON
Polynikes!
How did you sneak in?

POLYNIKES
I lived in Thebes my whole life,
I know all the tactical wall breaches.

HÆMON
Now that I smell you,
I can tell you came through the sewers.

POLYNIKES
I did, yes.

(POLYNIKES goes offstage then re-enters with cans of BetaMaxx®, he pops one open)

POLYNIKES
Hey, what did Antigone say about matrimony?

HÆMON
She said she'd think about it.

POLYNIKES
I tell you, being married is pretty great.
Giving your soul to another person to guard, is in the top-thirteen reasons to live.

HÆMON
But you're not married, Polynikes.

POLYNIKES
Yes, I am, to Argea,
She is really quite the catch.
Want to see a picture?

(POLYNIKES takes out another picture torn from a periodical)

HÆMON
This is from a kayaking magazine.

POLYNIKES
Yeah, doesn't my wife look great in a life-vest?

(Enter ETEOKLES dressed like a historical Emperess, wearing the Coat of Thebes)

ETEOKLES
Aha!
My trap worked.

POLYNIKES
What trap, Eteokles?

ETEOKLES
I knew if I kept the royal pantry well stocked with BetaMaxx®.
I would finally catch you stealing it, Polynikes.
Since Kreon failed in Athens claiming our Father,
I knew I needed to take my legacy into my historical hands.
Sind Sie bereit, Ihr Tod, twin treffen ich?

POLYNIKES
What the ick was that?

HÆMON
Eteokles is learning German.

ETEOKLES
All the great leaders speak Deutsch.

POLYNIKES *(interested)*
Really?

ETEOKLES
Ja.
But I asked, are you ready to meet your death, Twin?

POLYNIKES
Oh, the death I will meet will be yours, Germophile.

(ETEOKLES and POLYNIKES wrestle very sloppily)

ETEOKLES
I will be recognized as the greatest Theban ruler in history.

POLYNIKES
The Coat is rightfully mine,
As the eldest child.

ETEOKLES
Um elf Sekunden.

POLYNIKES
You're an elf.

HÆMON
Stop it, twins, this fight is embarrassing.

(POLYNIKES and ETEOKLES stop wrestling)

POLYNIKES
Hæmon's right, this fight... not good.
I'm spilling my BetaMaxx®.
Plus, if I kill you here, my army will be alienated from the
    honor.

HÆMON
Why don't you fools match the .07 against Agamemnon and
    his Champions of Thebes.
You two can face off yourselves,
A few against a few in a fight fair finally!
Get it over and stop embarrassing yourselves along with
    this whole city.
Merry Dragon Day, you dumbells.

(Exit HÆMON)

POLYNIKES
Is it Dragon Day?

ETEOKLES
I guess it is, Twin.

POLYNIKES
We used to love Dragon Day.

ETEOKLES
We did.

POLYNIKES
Well, Merry Dragon Day.

ETEOKLES
Frohe Morgen des Drachen.

(POLYNIKES and ETEOKLES awkwardly shake hands)

POLYNIKES
Hæmon's a boob, but his idea of a few on few seems
    compelling,
I'm sure my .07 will go for it.

ETEOKLES
I know Agamemnon and his Champions are well trained in
    single combat,
While your skippers are well trained in sloth and profanity.

POLYNIKES
If you're so sure you'll win,
Let's do it.

ETEOKLES
Let's.
Go get your mayflies and minions,
And Thebes shall battle your lambkins.
This could be over in time for my dinner date.

POLYNIKES
If your dinner date be with the worms,
Then ye shall make it.

(Enter KREON)

KREON
Hail Eteokles, Empress of Thebes.

POLYNIKES
Look Kreon, a red panda.

(Exit POLYNIKES hurriedly)

KREON
Why did Polynikes point at an imaginary red panda?

ETEOKLES
Who knows.

(POLYNIKES enters, gets more BetaMaxx®, then he re-exits)

ETEOKLES
Because you failed in convincing my father to return,
I must now engage within a fair Few against Few,
In single combat to spare our people, time, and money.
All of which I value.

KREON
What of your life?

ETEOKLES
Oh, I will not pay that price, Uncle Kreon,
I shall be Thebes' Champion, her Champion Empress,
Slaying the Dragon as Cadmus had done.
Oh, my blade shall ease into Polynikes' heart,
And the people will love me all over again.
This be the finest chapter of my biography, Kreon,
Can you picture the illustrations of this battle!
The blood spray on my face from my fallen brother, the
    savage invader.
Thebes will see their Empress provided safety unequaled.
And the lovers, those uncontrolled bundles of passion.
Oh, the lovers, Uncle Kreon, I will be known for.
Der lockige Sex wirkt wie Honig.

KREON
I'm not sure what you just said, my Emperess,
But if I may speak truthfully, I worry not for Captain
Agamemnon or his Champions,
I'm confident they'll triumph over the .07.
But niece, you have never fought in a battle,
Nor have you trained.

ETEOKLES
You bring up some valid points,
I am a little wie eine Wurst.
If I die, then the Coat is yours.

KREON
Empress, I do not want the Coat.
Especially after your leadership.
It's a tough era to follow.

ETEOKLES
Fine, if I die give the Coat to Viceroy Thíba,
And demand she carry out my last order,
Do not grant burial respect to Polynikes,
Let him rot with the sewerage of Thebes.
Lassen Sie ihn in der Scheiße verrotten!

KREON
That seems extreme.

ETEOKLES
Especially in German, right?
Under no circumstance are we to let Polynikes be buried,
That would be a disaster to public order.

KREON
What about the age-old Theban proverb:
The dust of the past cannot settle,
Without a burial.

ETEOKLES
That fits not into my legacy, so I'd like it struck from the records.
Help Thíba make that rebel suffer shame,
Let him lie among the city's refuse.
Lassen Sie ihn in der Scheiße verrotten!

KREON
Okay, I will always obey my Empress.

ETEOKLES
That's what I like about you uncle.
I go to prepare for fighting.

KREON
One second, you had me call Tiresias for some forecasts,
She's arrived.

ETEOKLES
I forgot I did that.
I tell you, she gives me the creeps.

KREON
But she always has solid advice.

ETEOKLES
But does it need to be creepy advice?

(Enter TIRESIAS)

TIRESIAS
I got bored waiting.

KREON
Tiresias, your prediction may be easier than planned.
Eteokles prepares for single combat against her rebellious
  brother,
We're sure of victory.

TIRESIAS
Well, Kreon, if you're all so certain, I won't bother you
with the truth of what I see.

ETEOKLES
Great, thanks for coming.
Maybe we can get her some sauerbraten or something.

KREON
Wait, Tiresias, tell me if you see a vision.

(KREON grabs TIRESIAS)

TIRESIAS
I hate being touched by your cheese-covered hands.

KREON
Sorry, sorry.

TIRESIAS
Tell me Kreon, will you enact anything I speak,
If I say the manner in which you can save Thebes will you
    take as truth my prediction?

KREON
I would do anything to secure Thebes.

TIRESIAS
Where's Hæmon, my little stewpot friend?

KREON
Probably fawning over Antigone.

TIRESIAS
He can, along with his adoptive father, be the hero of
    Thebes.

KREON
Hæmon has no heroic desires.

TIRESIAS
It is not his desire I question but yours.

ETEOKLES
Just out with it, Frauline, some of us have a busy day here.

TIRESIAS
Kreon, our Hæmon must play the role of the Dragon that
  Cadmus slew,
And the role of Cadmus need be played by you.

KREON
What does that mean?

TIRESIAS
Kreon, Thebes shall finally find peace tomorrow.

KREON
That's great.

TIRESIAS
When you take the life of that boy we both love.
Kreon kills Hæmon.

KREON
I kill Hæmon?

TIRESIAS
Yes, Kreon, you do, tomorrow.
So are you glad you called?

ETEOKLES
Enough, you thing with no vision.
You come to haunt,
You come to infect with fear,
You sow hate and reap revenge.
You spread lies like children spread Marmelade auf Brot.
Leave us, you grudging gazer of message ghoulish.
You, who are loosed from gaudy recess of garish hell.
Geh, geh!

TIRESIAS
Kreon, remember that night,
Before we fell apart,
Standing on the pier,

The warm air from the sea,
And you had wished that we could die together?

KREON
I remember.

TIRESIAS
Might still happen, honey.

(Exit TIRESIAS)

ETEOKLES
Don't fret, Uncle, the Theban Champions will defeat the
   Ei-Schichten of Polynikes.

KREON
I've got to send my Hæmon from Thebes.

(ETEOKLES exits, passing HÆMON with his tortoise)

HÆMON
Papa.

KREON
My son. You must leave me, leave Thebes, now.

HÆMON
Leave Thebes?
I could never, I love you, I love Thebes.

KREON
Thebes loves you not son, you and Cadmusaurus must go,
Tiresias gave us a prophecy.

HÆMON
Tieresias says I leave Thebes?

KREON
In so many words, yes.
You must be gone by tomorrow.

HÆMON
You must've misunderstood,
I'm not going anywhere, I asked Antigone to marry me.

KREON
You're too weak for Antigone.
She'll never love you, foolish kid, leave her behind.

(Enter ANTIGONE)

ANTIGONE
What's going on?

KREON
Antigone, as with all your life, you arrive just in time to complicate affairs.

HÆMON
Papa says you'll never love me.

KREON
You know it's true, don't toy with his heart.

ANTIGONE
Actually, I love Hæmon.
I will mary him!

HÆMON
Really?

KREON
Hæmon, she manipulates you, it's antagonism against me.

HÆMON
Curse not my fortune, Father, because you yourself have none.
I am marrying the woman I love, have happiness for me.

KREON
Hæmon, I can have happiness for you, but I cannot lose you.

HÆMON
You just lost me, Old Man.
Maybe that's the prophecy Tiresias was trying to convey,
That you drive me from your heart.

ANTIGONE
Come on, let's plan our wedding.

(Exit HÆMON and ANTIGONE passing ETEOKLES armed pompously for battle in a different historical outfit)

HÆMON *(Exiting)*
We're getting married!

ETEOKLES *(Calling after)*
Why are you so mad about it?
What is wrong with this family?

KREON
Look niece, I'll take the Coat if you die, I'll take the Coat.
I will not fail Thebes again.

ETEOKLES
Why the change of Geist?

KREON
Because if a king says go, gone ye shall be.

ETEOKLES
It's true uncle, History can teach us all.
Und der Mond gießt Suppe.

KREON
No disrespect intended,
But I don't think you're ready to have conversations in
  German.

(Enter POLYNIKES on his child's bike, followed by KAPANEÚS, TYDEUS and two other .07ers, carrying random items for weapons)

ETEOKLES + KREON
Polynikes!

(POLYNIKES attempts many free-styling tricks. The .07 chants)

POLYNIKES
Hello, little twin.

ETEOKLES
So nice of you to bring such noble captains.

KAPANEÚS
Calls us the .07, Empress.

TYDEUS
Empress of my crap!

ETEOKLES
Clever, classy, thank you Twin, you really bless the line of
  Cadmus.
I'm sure Captain Agamemnon and his Champions will be
  charmed to meet you.

POLYNIKES
Where is this great Captain Agamemnon?

ETEOKLES
He's just running his troupe through some exercises.

POLYNIKES *(laughing)*
Oh, exercises.

ETEOKLES
I don't think exercises are funny.

POLYNIKES *(laughing)*
We do... exercises.

ETEOKLES
May you greet doom with such spirits, brother mine.
Oh, by the way, Ich nenne ein Waffenstillstand.

KAPANEÚS
That's German for truce!
Huzzah, they be cowards. Thebes calls a truce!

.07ERS
Truce, truce, truce!

ETEOKLES
Yes, a truce... from calmness,
A truce... from civility,
A truce from pity.

POLYNIKES
Twin have we come to play with words?

ETEOKLES
No twin, we've come to play with ssss-words.

POLYNIKES
Bring forth Agamemnon and your Champions,
However weak they be.

ETEOKLES
Methinks me-hear them come.

(Enter AGAMEMNON and his THEBAN CHAMPIONS: ΦILOKTETES, ODYSSA and MENELAUS. They all scream and rush onstage with incredible precision and military order)

THEBAN CHAMPIONS
Long live the Emprehhhhhhss!

TYDEUS
Holy shin guard!

AGAMEMNON
Draw!

(The THEBAN CHAMPIONS all draw huge shiny swords)

TYDEUS
Look at those ssswords.

POLYNIKES
Stay true, .07ers, we have the righter cause.

KAPANEÚS
And what might that cause be, Polynikes?

(POLYNIKES shrugs)

ETEOKLES
Uncle Kreon, hold the Coat of Thebes for me, until I kill
  my brother,
And remember my decree.

(ETEOKLES gives the Coat of Thebes to KREON)

KREON
Lassen Sie ihn in der Scheiße verrotten.

ETEOKLES
That's right, let Polynikes rot in the sewerage.
Scribe! Make sure this is registered.
(Speaks to the sky, as if to a recording device)
You see ruling is a Brise,
Just think of yourself like an alien,
With stainless internal gadgets,
And the people need the magic of those gadgets,
Then give it to them
Give them that magic,
Until their brains turn to sugar,
Through the magic of your gadgets.
Angreifen!

*(ETEOKLES, AGAMEMNON, ΦILOKTETES, ODYSSA
and MENELAUS attack POLYNIKES and the four .07ERS.
The ODD-JOBS sing)*

[THE SONG OF THE UNFAIR BATTLE]

(As expected, the .07ERS fall quickly. Some of them die offstage. An ODD-JOB crosses the .07 off on the board and tallies four deaths. ETEOKLES and POLYNIKES continue to fight horribly)

AGAMEMNON
You need you some help, Empress Eteokles?

ETEOKLES
No thanks Agamemnon, I think I got it.

(ETEOKLES stabs POLYNIKES in a pretty bad place, physically)

ETEOKLES
Ja! Ja!

(ETEOKLES then holds her arms up in a victory stance. POLYNIKES, of course, runs her through)

POLYNIKES
Polynikes!

KREON
Saw that coming.

ETEOKLES
Dumm Pferd Gesicht, look what you did to us.

POLYNIKES
This was...done...like long ago.
This is our father's inheritance of pain and death.
Tell my wife, Argea, I love her.

ETEOKLES
I am dying too fool.
And she doesn't even exist.

POLYNIKES
But I love my wife.

KREON
I will tell her for you, Polynikes.

POLYNIKES
Thank you uncle.
Good bye, Emprsssssss.

ETEOKLES
Yeah, see you, brother, my epic was shorter than I thought.
Merry Dragon Day.

POLYNIKES
Merry Dragon Day.

ETEOKLES
Ich liebe dich.

*(POLYNIKES and ETEOKLES die. An ODD-JOB crosses
their names off and tallies their deaths)*

AGAMEMNON
Who rules now?

KREON
This guy.

(KREON puts on the Coat of Thebes)

CHAMPIONS
Long live King of Thebes Kreon!
Long live Kreon!

KREON
Okay, okay, settle down.

AGAMEMNON
King Kreon, can we Theban Guard be dismissed?
Thebes obviously no longer needs us, I'm sure there is some
  fight somewhere to be had.

MENELAUS
Plus, I'm not a fan of the tea selection here.

KREON
Sure, go ahead.
But first, deliver the dead Empressto the morgue,
Take the .07 to their families.

(AGAMEMNON and MENELAUS clear off ETEOKLES.
ODYSSA and ΦILOKTETES start clearing the dead .07ERS.
ANTIGONE and HÆMON enter)

ANTIGONE
I shake by the power of loss,
The Twins have stolen life from the other.

KREON
Come on Antigone, these stupid kids longed for this,
No need to mourn them.

HÆMON
How could she not mourn her kin?

KREON
By knowing they were wrong.

ANTIGONE
The only wrong I see here is you wearing the Coat,
Kreon.

KREON
Right, of course, always right, Antigone.
"I'm Antigone, I'm always right."
Well good news Hæmon,
Your king is allowing your marriage.
See rise the sun, see dawn your wedding day.
Come lunch, you'll be espoused to that happy chuck, with
  tears on her face.
Then you both must quit the land, with your tortoise.
Thebes welcomes none of you.
So it's decreed by your new king, lord and sire, Kreon.

ANTIGONE
I would rather die than leave this land again.

KREON
Taunt not death girl, you see how much he likes to taste your blood.
Get along, I can no longer stand your faces.

HÆMON
Is this about Tiresias' prediction?

KREON
It is about me being king.
And the reason of your king is all the sense this world needs.

ANTIGONE
We'll figure it out later Hæmon.
Help me with Polynikes, we'll dig a grave and honor him.

KREON
No no no, back away from that body.
Hear ye all, touching Dead Polynikes is now punishable by death!

ANTIGONE
Anger against the dead only harms the living.

KREON
It was Eteokles' last decree before succumbing to sororicide,
Lassen Sie ihn in der Scheiße verrotten.
Let my brother rot in sewerage, call she.

HÆMON
You're a fool to enforce that edict.

KREON
If fools follow laws then only fools crave justice.
We must heed the orders of rulers inappropriate or not.

ANTIGONE
The dust of the past cannot settle without a burial.

KREON
The past is past and I am now your king.

ANTIGONE
Well, King, you stink.

KREON
Oh, does justice smell?

ANTIGONE
Yes, like unwashed clothes of gymnasiums,
And cheap cheesy-snacks.

(AGAMEMNON and MENELAUS enter)

KREON
Agamemnon, take dead Polynikes to rot in the sewer,
And yours shall be the last lawful hands to touch him.

AGAMEMNON
Uck.

(AGAMEMNON and MENELAUS exit with DEAD POLYNIKES)

ANTIGONE
Hey King, can you hear me?

KREON
Yes, your king can hear.

ANTIGONE
Then my king hears me say, I will bury my brother.

KREON
Then your king hears you lie,
Because that tumor will be left to bloat in the refuse of
  Thebes.

ANTIGONE
I will bury Polynikes.

KREON
Will you?

ANTIGONE
Aye.

KREON
Then you will die.

ANTIGONE
Why stop what is to come?

(Exit ANTIGONE)

KREON
Pick out a wedding dress, Antigone!
And pack your biggest bags!
No room for you or your one-hour come groom!
Says the new King of Thebes.

HÆMON
Oh, inhabitants of this unhappy land,
Forsaken, inglorious in misery, I weep for us.
For this bounty did King Cadmus slay the Dragon?
For this bounty did Œdipus solve the riddle of the Hellbitch?

KREON
That was awesome.

HÆMON
How did I turn out so well adjusted?

KREON
You're saved son, in ways you will never see,
This whole city is saved,
We can all wipe the past clean and move on,
March into the future,
Please, please, let's leave the past,
To be eaten by the rapacious dogs of yesteryear.

Just leave Thebes and we're all saved,
We're all saved from a horrendous incursion of an
obscene wave,
We are saved,
We are saved,
We are saved.

(Exit KREON)

HÆMON
"I hate life."
Oh, Cadmusaurus, don't think like that,
It almost has to get better.

(Exit HÆMON)

ODD-JOB SOAPY
Sunday Morning, year 50:
Antigone.

(Enter AGAMEMNON, ΦILOKTETES, ODYSSA and MENELAUS carrying DEAD POLYNIKES. They drop him on sludge)

MENELAUS
So this is where all our crap goes.

AGAMEMNON
Uck, stinks.

(KALCHAS, comes from the trap, they've been living in the sewer)

KALCHAS
Aaaaah-xcuse me.

GREEKS
Ah!

KALCHAS
Sorry for troubles!
I am interrupting, right?

I am Kalchas.
I have been waiting here to say something,
I don't even know where I am.

AGAMEMNON
The sewers of Thebes, kid.

KALCHAS
Yes, that's it.
The bats said to me,
"Hi-yo to sewers of Thebes."
After my mother died a few weeks past my ear was bitten
  by a bat,
Since then, the bats are able to ssquek me their dreams of
  the future unfolding.
These bat-squeak-dreams are clear in their images,
But not always in their meaning, unclear.

(KALCHAS shows a gross, infected ear)

ODYSSA
Truthfully, you should seek some medical help for that ear.

KALCHAS
Don't wah medical help,
I'm ascared if my ear heals,
Thc bats will stop squeaking their fantasies.
I must come here, crap of Thebes, so show the bats, through
  my ear.
Eeek eek eek.
I need to speak with Phillip Teddies.

ΦILOKTETES
Φiloktetes?

KALCHAS
Yes, Phillip Teddies.
Bats say I must be his friend.
Phillip Teddies, Phillip Teddies.

ΦILOKTETES
I'm Φiloktetes, kid.

(KALCHAS hugs ΦILOKTETES)

KALCHAS
Phillip Teddies, we'll be pals.
Get Agamemnon.

AGAMEMNON
I'm Agamemnon.

KALCHAS
Scary man.
Agamemnon, get your brother Menelaus.

MENELAUS
I'm Menelaus.
I'm married to Helen with her prized looks.

KALCHAS
Eeek eek eek.
More on that later.
Get Odyssa.

ODYSSA
Hollah.

KALCHAS
Get Ajax and Achilles.

ΦILOKTETES
Ajax and Achilles are great warriors,
Like slightly younger versions of Herakles,
Not as glorious, but about as close as you can get,
nowadays.

KALCHAS
Get them later.
Then Phillip Teddies take us all to Port of Pride.

Greek forces will gather eek and wait to sail to Troy.
There is going to be a war,
Unlike any other war,
That has warred on war.
So squeak the bats,
Through my ear.

ΦILOKTETES
Did you know the city of Troy,
Used to be called Old Troad,
And Herakles single-handedly defended that city.

AGAMEMNON
I knew that, yes.

ODYSSA
What's in Troy, Kalchas?

KALCHAS
Menelaus' wife.

MENELAUS
My wife, Helen?

KALCHAS
Yes, Seven Sister Helen, full of face, stolen by Princely
Paris.

MENELAUS
My Helen was kidnapped?

KALCHAS
Not quite kidnapped but went with willingly,
Let's a go and get her back.
Ho ho we go. A go, ho, a go. Eeek eek.

(KALCHAS skips off)

MENELAUS
My wife Helen left me?

AGAMEMNON
If that child speaks true, we should call on the war-pact of
  Helen's wooers,
And send all of Greece to war.

MENELAUS
Maybe we can negotiate with Troy, Agamemnon.

AGAMEMNON
Nope, it'll have to be war.
Let's go.

ΦILOKTETES
It's going to be an adventure.
Let's see, do I have everything?
I got the Palladium Bow, I got my lucky fur-cap.

(ΦILOKTETES shows his furry hat)

ODYSSA
That's clearly a wig.

ΦILOKTETES
Okay, Odyssa, it's not a wig.

ODYSSA
It looks like a wig.

MENELAUS
It does look like a wig.

ΦILOKTETES
It's not a wig.

(Enter KALCHAS)

KALCHAS
Bats think it's a wig.

ΦILOKTETES
What do bats know?

KALCHAS
Tons.
Oh Phillip Teddies, careful of snakes and feet,
The Port of Pride is lousy with snakes.

ΦILOKTETES
I hate snakes a heckuvalot,
But with the Palladium Bow of Herakles, what need I fear
  snakes?
Ha-hey!

*(ΦILOKTETES waits for people to know what, "Ha hey"
means. They don't)*

AGAMEMNON
What's ha-hey?

ΦILOKTETES
Just something my friend used to say.

*(ANTIGONE enters wearing a wedding-dress, carrying a
shovel and a large power-drill)*

ANTIGONE
Theban Champions.

ODYSSA
Ma'am.

ANTIGONE
Are you all going to stop me?

AGAMEMNON
Let Kreon deal with you, it's not our fight.
We go to Port of Pride, set sail to Troy.

MENELAUS
I'm a little shocked my wife left me.

AGAMEMNON
We'll get her prized-head back for you in no time, brother,
I mean how long could this war last?

(Exit AGAMEMNON, ΦILOKTETES, ODYSSA and MENELAUS)

KALCHAS
It lasts a while.

(Exit KALCHAS)

ANTIGONE
Hello, Polynikes.

(ANTIGONE climbs into the trap and starts digging. The stage starts gathering dirt and sludge. KREON enters in the Coat of Thebes over a tux, drinking Dragon-Head Coffee®)

KREON
You know, I actually thought you weren't going to do this.

ANTIGONE
Hey Kreon, looking good.

KREON
I saw you radiant in your wedding dress.

ANTIGONE
Thank you.

KREON
I actually thought, maybe once in her life Antigone will take the easy aisle.
Maybe once she'll seek joy and peace,
Rather than trying to right all the wrongs of the world.
Maybe just this once, on her wedding day,
Antigone will act like all the other young women of the world.
But then an hour passes, we're all waiting by the altar,

Two, three hours, and I knew, I should come to the sewer,
And sure enough, here you are.

ANTIGONE
Sure enough.
The dust of the past cannot settle without a burial.
Under a sewer is not ideal, but hey, we're all here now.

KREON
Everyone's at the wedding, waiting,
I think even Theseus showed up.

ANTIGONE
So they'll wait.
There's a DJ, right.

KREON
Yes there is, and not a cheap one either.
Boy, it's hot down in here.

(KREON takes off the Coat of Thebes)

ANTIGONE
It's the decomposition of everything the city flushed away,
Including Polynikes.

KREON
Do you still want to marry Hæmon?
You called for this wedding, I said no, you were all like yes,
   I love him.

ANTIGONE
I know I'm breaking Hæmon's heart.
I'm not proud about that.

KREON
Wouldn't it have been easier to just marry him,
And take him from Thebes like I demanded,
Rather than all this hard work.

ANTIGONE
Easier, sure.
But there's reward in hard work.

KREON
Do you even know what you're doing?
Is this a power-drill?

(KREON picks up a power-drill and starts it whirring)

ANTIGONE
I thought I might need the drill,
In case you locked me down here.

KREON
Lock you down here?
What do you take me for?
I would not lock you in a sewer, Antigone.

ANTIGONE
Well, I didn't know.

KREON
How about a deal?
You marry Hæmon, then hand in hand, walk away from
   Thebes.
And I'll bury Polynikes.

ANTIGONE
Would Thebes allow that?

KREON
Thebes wouldn't need to know family secrets.

*(THÍBA enters dressed in a military uniform of the Bacchae
Politcal Party, with her umbrella, drinking some Dragon-
Head Coffee®, she is no longer sick)*

THÍBA
Ring a ring, King Kreon.

KREON
Stepmother Thíba.

THÍBA
When the Bachae learned you took the Coat of Thebes, we
held an emergency meeting.
We got you a card.

(THÍBA gives KREON a card)

KREON
Thank you, Viceroy.

THÍBA
Thank you, King.

ANTIGONE
Nice Fox outfit.

THÍBA
I love the way it fits.
I'm so glad I can see these glory days for my namesake city,
my Thebes.
All thanks to Eteokles, our Empress, may her history be
written well.
Remember I wanted Cadmus to kill me?
Ha!
We'll be right outside.

(THÍBA salutes then exits)

ANTIGONE
It's creepy to me how old that woman is,
Could be like my great-grandmother or something,
She looks younger than me.

KREON
All those Seven Sisters age half as fast as us.
What a gift right?

ANTIGONE
A life twice as long?
No thanks.
What's the card say?

KREON
It's a Father's Day card. How odd?
"King Kreon, the population of Thebes sees you as a selfish
  usurper,
No better than Pentheus the Gaunt,
Allow the burial of Polynikes and suffer execution at the
  hands of Viceroy Thíba,
Thebes' true ruler.
With love, the Bacchae."

ANTIGONE
Yikes, there goes our family secrets.

(KREON sets up the card on the ground)

KREON
When I was banished the first time,
Cadmus asked me is it best to be friendly, feared or
  faithful?

ANTIGONE
I think about that all the time.

KREON
Do you have an answer?

ANTIGONE
Faithful.

KREON
You're always certain.

ANTIGONE
Your opinion?

KREON
I used to think friendly.
But I have to make decisions for people you know,
What gives me the right.
King Kreon, it even sounds ridiculous.

ANTIGONE
I heard worse.

KREON
Truth is, I accepted the Coat because I thought, as King,
I could save Hæmon from one of Tiresias' prophecies.

ANTIGONE
Has that Coat ever brought good fortune to anyone?

KREON
No, but a man must hope even when hope makes it hard.

ANTIGONE
So what's your opinion now?
Is it best to be friendly, feared or faithful?

KREON
If I had to commit,
I would say... feared.
It's the easiest way to get people to obey laws.

ANTIGONE
You think if you frighten me, I'll obey your law?

KREON
Iron gives way to fire, wild horses become docile playthings.
Family must yield to state.

ANTIGONE
I'm not so sure, Uncle.

KREON
Because you are a hateful woman.

ANTIGONE
What have I ever done out of hate?
In spite of everything, I only love.
I stay open for love and the world debases me,
Then I open for love again.

KREON
Look, I'm starving, you can take a rest, right?
I promise, no tricks.
Break bread with your family here.

ANTIGONE
What food you got, Uncle?

KREON
I bet you can guess.

ANTIGONE
Cheezee-Q's®.

(KREON pulls out a half-eaten bag of Cheezee-Q's®)

KREON
I love these things.

ANTIGONE
Everyone knows you do.
Got any water?

KREON
Nope only a Dragon-Head® coffee.

(ANTIGONE stops working and eats with KREON)

KREON
I just passed Captain Agamemnon, he's going to lead an
    army to fight in Troy.
All because his Seven Sister-in-Law was seduced.
He looked so confident, but he'll see troubles, leading men
    to war over love.

ANTIGONE
I don't think love could cause a war.
I think people fight because we're corrupt harbingers of selfish desires.
We want to destroy what others have just because we can.
We're all fools chasing around toy-trains of other fools.
We kill one boy to get his train but that train gets snatched by another boy
So we kill again to retrieve it.
We're idiots killing idiots because we've got nothing else to do,
And we can.
We make nations that tell us it's okay to kill other nations,
And we think our Patriotics is better than the Patriotics of others.
   But in truth, our nationality is just a few poetic words on an old piece of paper,
So, many die—soldiers, children, sick, old, animals, guilty, mad, simple, sad,
All killed,
For what?
For love?
Wouldn't it be romantic if those tales of stolen devotion were true?
No, we fight, so that when others die,
They're less important than us.

(ANTIGONE and KREON finish eating in silence)

ANTIGONE
Thanks for the snack.

KREON
And the Dragon-Head® coffee.
Don't want to be ungrateful.

ANTIGONE
No I don't.
Grave's ready by the way.

KREON
So, we are there then?

ANTIGONE
Yes sir, we're there.
The dust of the past cannot settle without a burial.
Help me or kill me, Kreon.

KREON
Antigone, as soon as you touch Polynikes you pass your verdict.

ANTIGONE
You see I ask not all this crap to fly,
For without wings how can crap take flight?
I ask not stone for nutrients,
For stones cannot give what stones do not have,
Thus Kreon lacks the compassion to understand.

KREON
Oh no, finally I understand, I understand what you're doing, and why you're doing it.
And I understand, we're just on different ends of the understanding.

ANTIGONE
Bye-bye, Kreon, see the last steps I take.
See the last spots of mud that splash upon my face.
See me come and take death as my groom.
And then see Antigone no more!

KREON
Okay.

(ANTIGONE quickly grabs DEAD POLYNIKES. ODD-JOBS sing)

[THE DIRGE OF DIRT]

(KREON kicks ANTIGONE in the face and she falls into the grave. KREON then hits ANTIGONE with the shovel. KREON in a panic, closes the trap, then covers it with DEAD POLYNIKES. HÆMON in a tuxedo enters running without his tortoise)

HÆMON
Papa! What are you doing?

KREON
Hæmon, son, you can't be down here.
Nothing is here for you.
Hate me all you want but just leave Thebes.

HÆMON
I don't hate you,
I love you and I accept all that comes with that hardship.
Antigone!

(HÆMON tries to open the grave. KREON pushes him away)

ANTIGONE *(In covered grave)*
I am here Hæmon.

KREON
You can't save her.
So save yourself.

HÆMON
You make the laws and I obey?

KREON
Yes, right?
Is that wrong, Hæmon?
Is natural order screwed up?
Is it wrong that Fathers and Kings give structure to sons
  and subjects?
Is that wrong?
Antigone will soon die.
So abandon Thebes and start plowing less rocky fields.

HÆMON
You are a terrible person.

KREON
I know it stings.
I gave her a chance to leave Thebes with you.
She wouldn't.
I chose her death over yours, I would do the same again,
   again and again.
Antigone needs to die.

HÆMON
Then Antigone dies,
But when death visits, he never takes only one.

KREON
Is that a threat?

HÆMON
No sir, I'll happily dispatch from Thebes and you.

KREON
Thank you, son.

HÆMON
My pleasure, my King.
Good-bye Antigone.

ANTIGONE *(In grave)*
Hæmon, don't save me, this is right.

HÆMON
Yeah, I guess it is, Antigone.

(Exit HÆMON)

ANTIGONE *(In grave)*
Hæmon, I love you.
This choice was made for me long ago,
My life was always ghoulishly haunted by death.

Accept it, and find health, find an easy life.
I mean this, find things that can make you smile...

KREON
He's gone Antigone.

ANTIGONE *(In grave)*
What?

KREON
Hæmon is gone.
He's leaving Thebes.

ANTIGONE *(In grave)*
Oh.
Will you let me out then?

(Long pause)

KREON
No.

(Enter TIRESIAS. She looks radiant)

TIRESIAS
Our lives were long and filled with little reward,
We gave more pain than pleasure.
Didn't we, Kreon?

KREON
Wow Tiresias, you look beautiful.

TIRESIAS
I always dress up for funerals.

KREON
Whose funeral is it?

TIRESIAS
You'll see.
Do you ever take the time to consider the finer things of life?
Not the things gained by money but by choice.

KREON
Like what?

TIRESIAS
Love, promise,
Redemption.

KREON
I think about those things all the time.

TIRESIAS
Then you know better than to act this way.

KREON
What am I supposed to do?
Tell me, all-knower, what?

TIRESIAS
Bury Polynikes.
Pardon Antigone.

KREON
I can't.
I'm the king now.
I need to please this city, this horrible city I never even
   wanted to rule.

TIRESIAS
Please Kreon, see the betterment you can begin to build.

KREON
Tell me, love, please, in this better world you call for,
Does everyone all of a sudden become truthful, empathetic,
And act like they want to be treated?

TIRESIAS
No Kreon, I'm not talking about a betterment for the world,
The world will barely change by the actions of any one
person.

KREON
If not the world, then what, what can be better?

TIRESIAS
You can be better.
Make yourself better before we die.

KREON
Are we dying?

TIRESIAS
Were we ever not?

KREON
At least Hæmon escaped my murderous hands,
Ordered by his king safely away from your prediction.

TIRESIAS
You'll see.
Hey, back then, when we met,
When we were just kids in the bodies of adults,
Did you love me?

KREON
Tiresias, we were fools when we met.

TIRESIAS
(Drifting off) And still fools when we die.
I love this time of day,
When the sun wraps us all in soft warmth.
It's like the world becomes us,
And we become it.
Makes one happy to have shared life with a friend.

(TIRESIAS dies. An ODD-JOB crosses of her name and tallies her death)

KREON
I am sorry I left you.
When you love someone,
You should cherish her.

(The ODD-JOBS sing. HÆMON enters, puts his tortoise on the ground)

[*THE SONG OF LESS THAN HAPPY ENDINGS*]

HÆMON
Hello, Papa.

KREON
I thought you were leaving Thebes, Hæmon?

HÆMON
I'm freeing Cadmusaurus into the sewer.
Go on get out of here.
Go on!
No one wants you, baby dragon!

(HÆMON tries to nudge the tortoise offstage, it does not move. He picks up the power-drill sets it going)

KREON
Why?

HÆMON
Because I'm here to help Thebes settle the dust of the past,
And move on.
Oh great, Tiresias dead too.
In youth, Papa, I had so much promise, I thought I was
   going to be King.
By what action do we spend potential,
By what action does a life become so worthless?

(HÆMON pushes the power-drill into his brain. HÆMON collapses. KREON rushes to his body. An ODD-JOB crosses off his name and tallies his death)

KREON
No, son, no!
How did I kill my boy, how?

How, Tiresias how were you always right?
I have added nothing to the world,
Someone! Tell me where I went wrong!

(Enter THÍBA panicked, still dressed in her fox uniform)

THÍBA
Help me Kreon,
He's come back, he's mad from the Wasteland.

KREON
Who is, Thíba?

THÍBA
He's come back to settle the past,
He's come back to bury us,
To bury us all.
He's back to kill Thebes.

(In madness, CADMUS enters, looking crazed with a long white dirty beard, wearing tattered robes. He closes the sliding door)

KREON
Father? Cadmus?

THÍBA
Let me live, now we thrive,
End not Thebes with Seven Sister five.

(CADMUS picks up the shovel and bashes THÍBA's head. An ODD-JOB crosses off her name and tallies her death. KREON is silent, shocked. CADMUS then opens the trap flipping over POLYNIKES, he points. KREON looks into the pit)

KREON
Antigone?
Died so soon?

(An ODD-JOB crosses off ANTIGONE and tallies her death. CADMUS picks up the tortoise and puts it on its back. Cadmus takes the Coat of Thebes, ties one of the sleeve in a loop, he secures the other end to the wall, then puts the loop around his neck. CADMUS slides down the wall, slowly hanging himself, he start convuclsing. KREON watches)

KREON
Does anyone want our prayers?
Is there justice Father?
Is there?
Is it really so foolish to act against the corrosive powers of
    man that lie within us all?
Cruelty, selfishness, the ability to not sympathize,
Will be the certain death of everyone.
The dust of the past cannot settle without a burial.

(CADMUS stops convulsing. An ODD-JOB crosses of his name and tallies his death. KREON flips the tortoise right side up)

KREON
At least you'll make it out, little guy.

(KREON crawls into the grave)

KREON
Good-bye Thebes,
City founded on rotten death,
But then again, what city isn't?

(KREON shuts the trap on himself with a loud bang. Silence and ODD-JOB ERDIE crosses off KREON'S name)

ODD-JOB ERDIE
Is that it?

ODD-JOB SOAPY
Nope, there'll be more.

(ODD-JOB ERDIE tallies KREON'S death)

ODD-JOB ALICE
One-hour meal break.

(Lights fade over ODD-JOBS)

END OF
ALL OUR TRAGIC
ACT IV AND PART II

ABOUT THE PLAYWRIGHT

Sean Graney was the Founder and Artistic Director of the Hypocrites, a defunct Chicago theater company. He was the recipient of a Radcliffe Fellowship at Harvard University, a NEA/TCG Career Development Fellowship, a Creative Capital Grant and the Meier Achievement Award. Sean's work has been seen across the country including Oregon Shakespeare Festival, American Repertory Theatre, Berkeley Rep, and Actors Theater of Louisville. Sean received six Joseph Jefferson Awards for his directing and adaptation work. He currently lives in San Diego. He wants to thank you for your interest.

MORE PLAYS
ON SALE NOW FROM
SORDELET INK
WWW.SORDELETINK.COM

ACTION MOVIE: THE PLAY
JOE FOUST & RICHARD RAGSDALE

You want a play with a car chase, an alligator attack, and a bunch of super-cool fight scenes? Hoo boy, have we got something for you! When wiseacre supervillain John Kreegar gets his filthy mitts on an eldritch artifact of terrible power, everybody's ass is up for grabs! Luckily, the mysterious Dr. Xylene is putting together a fantastic team of good guys to fix Kreegar's wagon but good!

ALL CHILDISH THINGS
JOSEPH ZETTELMAIER

A heist comedy to warm the hearts of Star Wars fans! Dave Bullanski is planning the greatest heist ever. The idea is to take over an old Kenner warehouse and clean out all the rare Star Wars memorabilia, selling it off to a private collector willing to spend $2 million for the loot.

CAMPFIRE
JOSEPH ZETTELMAIER

A horror play. Marcus Carver has brought his niece and nephew back home. In the woods behind his farm, around a campfire, the Carvers will tell stories as they have for many generations. But a stranger has entered the dimly-lit circle.

CAPTAIN BLOOD
DAVID RICE

Unjustly sentenced to slavery on a Caribbean island, the bold Dr. Peter Blood falls in love with the lady of the plantation, the lovely Arabella Bishop. When Blood escapes and takes up the life of a pirate, it appears that fate has separated them forever...or has it? Filled with sword fights and pirate battles, love and treachery, and even a song or two, Captain Blood is a pirate adventure perfect for the whole crew!

CHURCHILL
RONALD KEATON

March 1946. After leading Britain and her Allies to victory in the European Theatre, Winston Churchill has been shockingly defeated for re-election as Prime Minister. Living in forced retirement, Churchill receives an invitation from President Harry Truman to speak at Westminster College in Fulton, Missouri, where he will deliver his legendary, emphatic "Iron Curtain" speech.

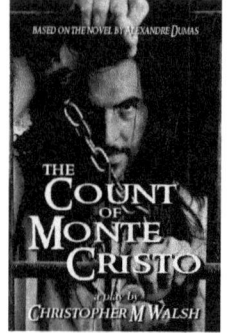

THE COUNT OF MONTE CRISTO
CHRISTOPHER M. WALSH

Framed by a conspiracy and torn from the woman he loves, Edmond Dantes is wrongly imprisoned for fourteen years. Escaping captivity, he enters the upper reaches of Parisian society, insinuating himself into the lives of his three tormentors as, one by one, he seeks to use their own secrets to destroy them in the guise of his new identity: the Count of Monte Cristo. A dark tale of intrigue and vengeance by epic storyteller Alexandre Dumas.

THE DECADE DANCE
JOSEPH ZETTELMAIER

A one-night stand becomes a ten-year journey as Rog and Nina navigate a relationship against the backdrop of a turbulent decade. A touching two-hander, carefully balancing nostalgia, romance, and humor as two people live unexpected lives.

DEAD MAN'S SHOES

JOSEPH ZETTELMAIER

A dark and hilarious western, with a dash of buddy-comedy. Notorious outlaw Injun Bill Picote has escaped from prison, along with a hard-luck drunk named Froggy. The unlikely partners endure trials and bizarre misadventures as they set out to right a terrible wrong.

DR. SEWARD'S DRACULA

JOSEPH ZETTELMAIER

Dr. Seward has cut himself off from the rest of the world after losing his lover and friends to Dracula. The Irish author Bram Stoker wishes to tell his story. Soon, a series of murders occur, very similar to the ones Seward fought to stop. A re-imagining of Bram Stoker's *Dracula*.

EBENEZER: A CHRISTMAS PLAY

JOSEPH ZETTELMAIER

It's a cold Christmas Eve in London, and Ebenezer Scrooge sits in a hospital room. 15 years have passed since his miraculous transformation by the Ghosts of Christmas. They are about to return for a final judgment. Based on Charles Dickens' classic *A Christmas Carol*.

EVE OF IDES

DAVID BLIXT

The night before his assassination at the hands of conspirators, Julius Caesar attended a feast. With him were Brutus, Cassius, and Antony. During the meal, Caesar was asked what he thought was the best way to die. Caesar answered, 'What does it matter, so long as it's quick?' Based on history and the works of Shakespeare, Eve Of Ides reveals the unexplored relationship between the main players of the age — Caesar, Brutus, and Antony.

FRANKENSTEIN

ROBERT KAUZLARIC

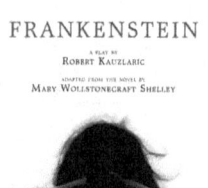

When an unexpected death shatters her family, Victoria retreats into the darkest recesses of her psyche in search of a way forward. To find meaning in this impossible loss, she brings a terrible creation to life — one whose existence threatens all hopes for the future. Haunted and hunted at every turn, Victoria must endure a nightmare journey of the soul in a quest for survival. A brilliant reimagining of the 1818 thriller by Mary Wollstonecraft Shelley.

HAUNTED

JOSEPH ZETTELMAIER

"The best way to know a place is through its ghosts." Michigan playwright Joseph Zettelmaier set out to collect a wide variety of ghost stories for this anthology play of true otherworldly encounters by Michiganders from Milan to Marquette.

HAWK'S TAVERN

LORI ROPER & RICK SORDELET

Hawks Tavern centers around estranged African American siblings who reunite amidst catastrophe. Together, they take on revolutionary measures while protecting the family bar amidst the tragic Newark riots of 1967. A bevy of family secrets set the stage for further turmoil in this comic-drama that which insists upon why we can't wait for social justice to heal the wounds suffered by the victimized.

HER MAJESTY'S WILL

ROBERT KAUZLARIC

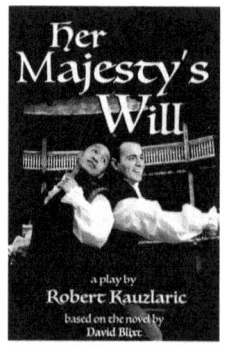

Young William Shakespeare is hiding from the law in rural Lancashire, languishing as a simple school master. Christopher Marlowe is living the high life as a spy for the Crown. When a dastardly plot to assassinate the Queen draws these two unforgettable wits together, Will is swept up in a world of intrigue, treachery, and mayhem in an adventure that will define the rest of his life — if he can only manage to survive it.

IT CAME FROM MARS
JOSEPH ZETTELMAIER

A hilarious look at the night of Orson Welles' famous *War Of The Worlds* broadcast! The members of Farlowe's Mystery Theatre Hour are in rehearsal for their weekly radio show when they hear an alarming announcement come over the radio—Martians have landed! Suddenly secrets are revealed as the cast and crew believe it is their last night on earth!

THE LEAGUE OF AWESOME
CORRBETTE PASKO & SARA SEVIGNY

The superheroes of The League Of Awesome have done it again. They decided to punish the SorrowMaker by trapping him inside a Hardy Boys book. Yeah, it was a little unconventional. Zoe, Sylvia, Penny, Kitty & Rumble wouldn't let him escape. I mean....come on! They'd have to be drunk to do that! Now let's watch them celebrate their victory over him with mojitos. Oh...oh dear.

MALAPERT LOVE
SIAH BERLATSKY

A hilarious mash-up/homage/reimagining of classical comedic elements! *Malapert Love* is a modern response to the tropes, style and structure of Shakespeare's comedies. It follows the tangled and farcical action of a group of people who have all fallen in love with the wrong person.

THE MAN-BEAST
JOSEPH ZETTELMAIER

The wilds of France are stalked by a fearsome creature—the Beast of Gévaudan. An outcast forester presents its corpse to King Louis for a rich reward. However, the story he told may not have been the entire truth. Based on the legends of the loupe-garou, the famous French warewolf.

THE MAN WHO WAS THURSDAY

BILAL DARDAI

When Gabriel Syme joins the undercover detail tasked with infiltrating an anarchists' operations, he soon finds himself sitting on their Supreme Council with the code name "Thursday." It slowly becomes clear that no one in this battle between law and chaos is as they seem — and that Scotland Yard may have created the very problem they're trying to solve. Uncover the truth in this absorbing adaptation of the 1908 satire by G. K. Chesterton.

THE MARK OF KANE

MARK PRACHT

In 1939, two young friends huddled in a Bronx apartment and created a legend, a caped crusader who represents an enduring chapter in the tale of the American comic book. One, Bob Kane, would profit from that legend for years to come. The other, Bill Finger, would be all but forgotten. This is the legacy of the mark of Kane.

THE MOONSTONE

ROBERT KAUZLARIC

The Moonstone, an Indian diamond steeped in a history of violence and mysticism, is stolen from Rachel Verinder's sitting room, and no one in her household is above suspicion. Join an unforgettable collection of liars, lovers, addicts and outcasts as they struggle to uncover the truth and reclaim the stone before its curse destroys them all. This thrilling mystery by Wilkie Collins is regarded as the first detective novel in the English language.

MY ITALY STORY/LONG GONE DADDY

JOSEPH GALLO

Spurred by visits from his grandmother's ghost, Thomas DaGato quits his job as a New York account executive, and travels to the tiny Italian village of his ancestors—Vallata. The sequel play chronicles the comic misadventures of becoming a stay-at-home father.

ONCE A PONZI TIME
JOE FOUST

For years, Harold has 'helped' his friends with their investments, but his artful dodging and shady shenanigans are about to collapse around him as his pyramid scheme tumbles to earth. With only the help of his flakey father, his naive nephew, and a ventriloquist's dummy, can Harold hoodwink the Russian mob, bamboozle the SEC, and restore his friends' fortunes without his entire world becoming a complete farce? Watch him try!

THE SCULLERY MAID
JOSEPH ZETTELMAIER

Having declared an uneasy truce in England's ongoing war with France, King Edward III and his nobles celebrate in Nottingham Castle. Unbeknownst to the king, a murder plot is being hatched in the kitchen by the lowliest of his servants, who seeks revenge to right the wrongs of a lifetime. Religion, politics, and questions of loyalty, all at a knife's edge.

ANTON CHEKHOV'S THE SEAGULL
JANICE L. BLIXT & ALEXANDRA LaCOMBE

This new translation of Anton Chekhov's classic The Seagull restores what most English-language versions of the play omit: humor. Considered a world-class humorist and wit, Chekov intended this play to be a Comedy. Translated by Alexandra LaCombe and adapted by award-winning director Janice L. Blixt, this is The Seagull audiences have been waiting for.

SEASON ON THE LINE
SHAWN PFAUTSCH

A novice assistant stage manager joins the crew of Bad Settlement Theatre Company for their make-or-break season. An aging artistic director is hell-bent on mounting the elusive perfect staging of Moby Dick. The play swings from soliloquy to action-adventure story as the young man grows to love the theatrical live, even a those around him pay the ultimate price for their pursuit of theatre's own great white whale.

A TALE OF TWO CITIES
CHRISTOPHER M. WALSH

The Reign of Terror sweeps through Paris, and two Londoners are confronted with impossible choices. Will aristocratic Charles Darnay abandon his family to protect an innocent man? Can depressive barrister Sydney Carton make the ultimate sacrifice for unrequited love? An epic story of resurrection and redemption, based on the 1859 novel by Charles Dickens.

THE TYRANT
RAFAEL SABATINI

Cesare Borgia, former cardinal, Duke of Valentinois and Romanga, tyrant and warlord, has been a figure of awe and scorn for generations. Famed author Rafael Sabatini (*Captain Blood, The Sea Hawk*) returned again and again to this fascinating historical figure's true nature, culminating it a romantic and treacherous piece of theatre.

VOICES IN THE DARK
JOSEPH ZETTELMAIER

Turn out the lights and shiver with delight at this anthology collection of seven short horror radio plays by renowned horror writer Joseph Zettelmaier.

WILLIAMSTON ANTHOLOGY
VOLUMES 1 & 2

Collecting the World Premiere plays from the first decade of The Williamston Theatre, this two-volume anthology celebrates life in the American Midwest with 14 original plays, ranging from comedy to classical, from romantic to horrific.

OTHER WORKS FROM
SORDELET INK
WWW.SORDELETINK.COM

HOLD, PLEASE
STAGE MANAGING A PANDEMIC
RICHARD HESTER

A pandemic chronicle from the particular point of view of a career Broadway stage manager living in Manhattan. Part journal, part blog, these essays attempted to make sense of the crisis and what it was doing to us. By the end, everything had changed. What follows is a journey through one of the most fascinating periods in both our cultural and our personal histories.

NELLIE BLY'S WORLD
VOL. 1 - 1887-1888

EDITED BY DAVID BLIXT

Bly's complete reporting, collected for the very first time! Starting with the stunt that made hers a household name, Nellie Bly spends her first year at the New York World going undercover to expose frauds, sharpsters and boodlers, interviewing Belva Lockwood and Hangman Joe, and tackling Phelps the Lobbyist!

NELLIE BLY'S WORLD
VOL. 2 - 1889-1890

EDITED BY DAVID BLIXT

Bly's complete reporting, collected for the very first time! Nellie buys a baby, has herself followed by a detective and arrested, interviews Helen Keller, champion boxer John Sullivan, and convicted would-be killer Eva Hamilton, all before setting out on her greatest stunt of all, a race around the world!

THE MYSTERY OF CENTRAL PARK

A rejected marriage proposal and the corpse of a dead beauty confound Dick Treadwell's hopes for happiness, until his beloved Penelope sets him a task: she will marry him if he solves— *the Mystery of Central Park!*

EVA, THE ADVENTURESS

Nellie Bly's ripped-from-the-headlines novel of a poor girl determined to revenge herself upon the world, only to find that, in the battle between love and revenge, only one can triumph.

NEW YORK BY NIGHT

Setting out to solve the bold diamond robbery, millionaire detective Lionel Dangerfield finds himself in competition with Ruby Sharpe, daring young reporter for the *New York Planet*. Will "The Danger" solve the case before Ruby can steal the story—and his heart?

ALTA LYNN, M.D.

A prank goes awry and Alta Lynn finds herself wed against her will. Leaving love behind, she throws herself into the study of medicine, only to find that love has other plans for her!

WAYNE'S FAITHFUL SWEETHEART

Beautiful Dorette Lover is rescued from poverty when she finds work as an artist's model. That same day she witnesses a seeming murder. To protect the man accused, she agrees to become his bride—only to fall desperately in love with him!

LITTLE LUCKIE

Luckie Thurlow longs to be accepted by society and gain the man she loves. But she harbors a dark secret—she is the daughter of the murderous Gypsy Queen, who plans to use Luckie to gain her own revenge!

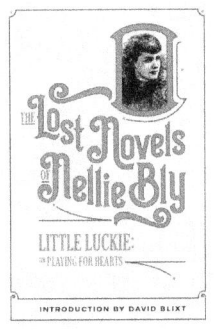

IN LOVE WITH A STRANGER

Kit Clarendon is in love! Trouble is, she doesn't know her love's name. But she is determined to track him down and force him to love her! A wild pursuit filled with disguises, desperate deeds, and declarations of love as Kit determines to go through fire and water to win him!

THE LOVE OF THREE GIRLS

An heiress in disguise, a factory girl with dreams of wealth, and a sweet child of charity are forced into rivalry when they all fall in love with the same man! Murder, fever, fallen women, and a desperate villain conspire against— *the love of three girls!*

LITTLE PENNY

Two young women must flee their troubled homes, forced into lives of hardship and poverty in New York City. Drawn together by fate, they soon become fierce allies in their shared struggle to build a happier future.

PRETTY MERRIBELLE

Trapped in a burning factory, pretty Merribelle's life is saved—but not her memory! A bizarre tale of amnesia, desperate love, and an even more desperate villain determined to use Merribelle to ruin his rival and achieve an inheritance worth millions!

TWINS AND RIVALS

Dimple and Della may be twins, but they have differing views on love. Dimple sees love as a contract, and marries for wealth to support her family, while Della longs to marry for love. The sisters collide when Dimple falls in love with Della's betrothed, turning them into rivals!

THE LOST NOVELS OF NELLIE BLY

ON SALE NOW FROM

SORDELET INK

WWW.SORDELETINK.COM